The Big Bonanza

~ *A Christian Fiction Novel*

Shakira R. Thompson

BELIEVER'S CHOICE
MEDIA

Shakira R. Thompson

Believer's Choice Media
P.O. Box 2131
Yulee, FL 32041
www.shakirabelieves.com

The Big Bonanza
Book Cover Designed by: Gad Savage

Library of Congress Congress Control Number: Applied For

ISBN: 978-0-9906725-5-5 (p); 978-0-9906725-6-2 (digital)

Scripture quotations are taken from the *Holy Bible, King James, The Amplified, Message, and Common English Bible Versions.*

Publisher's Note: *The Big Bonanza* is a work of fiction. All characters and places appearing in this work are fictitious. Any resemblance to real persons, living or dead, places, establishments, events, organizations, and/or locations is purely coincidental and a product of the author's mind.

First Printing, 2014

Shakira R. Thompson

To my ignition starter,
my guiding star,
and my little fire cracker.

Contents

Acknowledgements

Now that I've got gotten a few of these under my belt my list of acknowledgements all seem to remain the same. Nevertheless, I have to always thank the blessed Trinity for the work being done in my life. It is my desire that I work worthy of the vocation by which I've been called and that I become brighter and better as a result of my relationship with Christ. I pray that as you all read through my writings you will see my growth and the anointing present on each page.

This particular time I'd like to give a super duper special shout out to my family, The Thompsons, Sumlars, and Mitchells, Adams, and Blanchards for putting up with me while I'm working out my process. While I may appear that I'm not listening and get snappy when you voice your concern, I receive it all in the spirit in which it is being given and know that I love you all tremendously.

To my husband, Keith M. Thompson, you put up with it the most with me and for that I say thank you. May God bless you for your sacrifice in doing so. You and our daughters, my pride and joy mean the world to me and I wouldn't be able to do any of this without you guys.

I can't get away without thanking my graphic designer, my friend, Gad Savage who has proven to me over and over that I can trust again.

Thank you to all who believe in me; I'm truly grateful for all of your support. I'm blessed beyond measure and I thank you all for joining me on this road I'm traveling called life. No matter what, always remember to trust in the Lord. Thank you all and May God Bless.

Shakira R. Thompson

PROLOGUE

"Regina, why won't you stop packing? I don't understand what has gotten into you lately."

With each garment she packed, Bishop Montgomery unpacked it.

Without saying a word, Regina continued taking steps from her closet back to her bed, packing for her next speaking engagement.

"So are you just going to ignore me and pretend like you can't hear what I'm saying to you?"

Regina walked past her husband, she couldn't hold her silence any longer, "Stop unpacking my bag Eugene. When you say something worth my time, I'll respond."

Bishop Montgomery got up and blocked the entrance to Regina's closet, "How many times do I need to tell you, now is not the time for you to be leaving. Too much is going on for you to be going away. Ever since your little luncheon you've been going here and there with no consideration to me or what is going on with our church or our family."

Regina snapped back, "Now you take that back Eugene. I'm more than involved with what's going on at Wondrous Works. I've stood beside you for years, decades....why can't you support me a little huh? It's always about you Eugene, you, you, you, isn't that right?"

Bishop Montgomery huffed, "This is nonsense woman, I'm asking you not to go and that should be enough. It used to be enough, now nothing I say seems to matter to you anymore."

Regina pushed past her husband's barricade, she stepped back into her closet to grab more items.

Re-entering the bedroom she said, "Now why would you say something like that Eugene? You think because I've decided to expand my role of ministry beyond being your wife that nothing you say matters to me anymore? What does me leaving to go to a women's retreat to speak have to do with me not listening to you?"

Bishop Montgomery collapsed in the chevron chair tucked in the corner, "Women's retreat this weekend, prayer breakfast, the next weekend, ministry luncheon last weekend, I mean, when is it going to stop? We have some real issues going on right here and you're trapesing off to hither and yonder."

Regina stopped packing, narrowing her focus with her husband as the target, she laid it on heavy, "If I didn't know any better, I'd think you were jealous of me getting to go out and evangelize."

In a dismissive tone, Bishop Montgomery said, "Jealous…that's crazy talk woman. I'm trying to get you to understand that with our son's recent admission, we need to present a united front with every available opportunity we have. Not to mention the boy is sick….real sick. If you are always gone, how is that going to look to the congregation? We need to be strong and together during this time. I'm now faced with having to put off my retirement, there is no way Carson is fit or ready to lead this church. Let's not even begin talking about Courtney and Christian. Those two have only been married a month and they are already at each other's throats. I'm surprised their house is still standing with all that carrying on they've been doing over there. You know Cayden-James' appeal is coming up and how important that is. Honey, why can't you see you need to be here?"

Regina slammed her suitcase shut, "Eugene, no matter where I've been or what engagement I have coming up; I always make it back to Sunday morning service. Despite our sons being grown men, I'm here and will be here for them."

Bishop Montgomery held his hand to his chest and asked, "But what about me Regina? Who is going to be here for me? You certainly haven't been."

Sitting on top of the full luggage trying to zip it, Regina mocked her husband, "Who's going to be here for me? This is so typical. I've given you the best years of my life and the one time I get to be more than First Lady Regina, you now have a problem with that. You know what Eugene, let's just call these trips I've been taking what they are, breaks...breaks from each other. For the amount of time we've been in ministry, we've been able to move and grow together and here recently it feels we are growing in different directions."

Bishop Montgomery threw his hands up and exclaimed, "Yeah because you are going off on your own without me Regina."

First Lady Regina stomped off into the bathroom to grab her toiletry bag, walking back in, she began stuffing things into her shoulder bag. She looked over at her pouty mouth husband and asked, "How is going to preach the Gospel going off without you Eugene? You know, that's the part I can't seem to understand."

With dull eyes and a monotone voice, Bishop Montgomery's half-hearted shrug, indicated he was tired of arguing with his wife. He leaned forward with his elbows on his knees and said, "I promise to God, I don't think you need to go on this trip. Regina, I'm asking you, no, I'm begging you to stay but knowing you, you'll probably just ignore me and go anyway."

Regina lugged her bags next to the door, she turned to Bishop and said, "Honey...you just aren't being fair. Yes, I'm going but I'll be back before Sunday morning service."

Unwilling to offer any additional pleas, Bishop Montgomery issued parting words to his wife by saying, "Well then Regina you've made your choice so go ye therefore and teach all nations…go."

Bishop grabbed his keys from the nightstand, not only did he leave the room but he also left the house.

Regina breathed out a deep sigh, she calmed herself by picking up her bible and going over her notes for the upcoming message she would share.

CHAPTER 1

"Ahh, where has the time gone? I can't believe we only have a few more days left here in this beautiful paradise, I hope and pray, Monday takes its time getting here. How are you feeling about this weekend honey?"

Scarlett plopped herself on the bed, looking up at the bamboo ceiling fan twirl around and around, she said, "I'm not sure how I feel about much of anything these days. I guess you could say I'm nervous, scared, sick to my stomach, anxious, you name it and I'm all of those things."

"What do you mean you don't know much of anything these days?"

"James, how am I to be certain about ANYTHING these days considering all that is happening? Every time the phone rings, I'm thinking its Regina or Carson on the other end waiting to ask me about Chandler. I feel like I'm constantly looking over my shoulder, hoping Regina doesn't show up again like she did before. James, I live in constant fear that my baby is going to be taken away from me. I mean, I watched Carson stand before the church and confess to everything and he didn't even know I was there. What do you think he's going to do if he finds out about the baby? My God, I sat there looking at someone I didn't even recognize, I couldn't even believe he was once someone I was married to. He is really sick and I don't know what to do about it, if I should do anything at all. You know, everyone has an opinion about what I should do but I haven't really decided yet. My mind is so jumbled up right now, I can barely keep my thoughts together."

James walked over to the bed and sat next to Scarlett, stroking her arm, he said, "Well, are you saying you're uncertain about us? I mean, I've noticed you haven't been the same since we returned from California. I know you are afraid but sweetheart, I keep trying to tell you not to be. I'm not going to let anything happen to you or OUR son. I know you felt powerless against him before but you aren't that woman anymore. You possess more power than you realize honey. You know, I thought this trip might do us some good, will you look at this? We are in a gorgeous villa with the ocean waters below us. We are surrounded by all of God's beauty. I thought the allure of this tropical island would allure you back to me. I wanted you to be able to relax, hit up the spa, have a good time, and not have to think about anything but us and our little family but listening to you now...I'm not so sure."

Scarlett sat up, "James, you say you brought me on this trip for us but if that's the case why are all these other people here?"

Touching the base of his neck, James shook his head and asked, "What do you mean all these other people, you mean your parents? Honey, we have a new baby, you are a nursing mother, I think it's wonderful that George and Minta are able and willing to accompany us on a trip to help out with the baby so you and I can enjoy ourselves and still be able to take care of our son."

Scarlett snipped at James and said, "I'm not talking about them."

Scratching his head, James asked, "Are you upset Travis is here? Is that what this is all about? I told you before we left, George thought it would be good for all of us to go on a trip and when I suggested bringing you to Chee Chee Island, he thought it was a good idea. If Cole and Marissa didn't have finals, they'd be here too, would you feel the same way about them or are you just upset about Travis being here?"

"We just met him, I'm not sure I'm ready to be vacationing with him James."

James leaned into Scarlett, planting kisses down her arm and said, "He's your brother honey, maybe you should give him a chance and try to get to know him."

Crossing her arms, Scarlett said, "Hmm, you want me to give him a chance and get to know him when I barely know you. I mean, who knows you might end up turning out to be just like Carson for all I know."

Growing quiet, James thought, "*How could she say such a horrible thing to me? I should probably go before things get too far out of hand and we both say something we'll both regret.*"

Picking out a new pair of swimming shorts, James changed his clothes without saying a word, his chiseled body trembled slightly as a result of his wife's unkind and unfounded suspicions. James loved Scarlett and Chandler more than life, despite the short time they'd known one another, he fell in love and fell hard, she was the one for him, no question about it and time didn't need to tell him that. He'd promised to spend every day making her happy and seeing her smile and to see her in the current state she was in crushed him. He was feeling helpless at not being able to help his wife overcome her anxieties and insecurities.

Realizing the sting of her words carried more poison than she intended, Scarlett asked, "Where are you going?"

James pulled out his flip flops from under the bed, looked at Scarlett, and shook his head. He grabbed his phone and the room key and left, without answering.

Trying to process how such a beautiful morning had turned horrible so quickly, Scarlett jumped when the room phone rang, she slowly reached over and answered, "Hello."

"Good morning sunshine, how are you two love birds doing over there?"

Hearing little coos in the background of the phone call made Scarlett's icy heart melt, she could hear Chandler making the cutest noises through the phone. In an unexcitable tone, she answered her mother, "I've had better days, how are you?"

Minta's voice changed, "Oh lord, what does that mean? What's going on with you this morning?"

Scarlett confessed, "James and I just had a huge blow up. He left without even saying a word to me."

"What have you done to that man girl?"

"Mama? Are you taking his side over mine? Why are you assuming I did something to him?"

"Because I know you and I've learned him enough to know when he's upset, he just shuts down. So what happened?"

Scarlett filled in Minta on the morning's events, Minta confirmed, "I knew it….why would you say such a thing to him? Don't you know man's ego is fragile? Girl, James is nothing like Carson, in fact, he's the exact opposite. You have someone who loves you for you and your son in a nonthreatening way. Carson's blood may be flowing through Chandler but James is the real deal, the father who is putting in the day to day work with taking care of this little handsome angel here. You can play crazy if you want to, I'm sure there are plenty of women who would love to be married to that good doctor…just ask that 'ole, what's her name, yeah 'lil Miss Alicia. Yeah, ask her if you need to be reminded. When he comes back you need to make sure you apologize and show him how sorry you are. Did you hear what I said? I said show him, not just tell him."

"Jesus mama, you had to go there didn't you, but I get it, I hear you."

"Now, as your mother, I have to let you know that I'm concerned about you and what I've been seeing since you two came back from Wondrous Works. I may not have liked Carson very much but Regina and I had a pretty good relationship and I believe if she said she wasn't going to say anything then we should trust her at her word until proven otherwise. I can't imagine what you must be going through right now and how all of this is impacting you but as I've told you many times before, you have to trust God and believe everything is going to work out how it is supposed to. Now, since you've been back, I haven't seen you walking and talking. I know you are distracted honey but don't lose sight of what's important. You know what, right now, you're like an animal that gives off a stench to protect itself but honey your husband isn't your enemy."

Scarlett let out a big sigh, "As always, you are right. I have been very distracted and overwhelmed, my hormones are all out of whack...blame it on the hormones; I blame everything on the hormones. But you know what, you are right, I do need to get back on track. I know all things work together and I know I'm supposed to trust God to help me through and I've seen Him work miraculous things out in my life but sometimes it can be really hard to do that. I just find myself trying to figure out what to do next."

Minta switched ears as she adjusted Chandler on the bed, "Sweetheart listen, our human solutions do not compare to what God is able to do and solve for us. He's concerned about things that concern us so stop trying to figure everything out when you can hand it over to the ultimate problem-solver and way maker."

Smiling through the phone, Scarlett was beginning to feel a little better, she asked, "Hey listen, we got way off base, what were you calling for?"

"Well, I was calling to see if you were ready for me to bring Chandler over to you but I think you need to take a little more time for yourself. I have a little more milk here for him that you pumped last night so I'll call you back later. Maybe you should go for a walk and do a little talking with the Lord."

Both Minta and Scarlett snickered, Scarlett conceded, "I miss my baby, I'm ready to kiss those fat cheeks but I think I may go have a little walk and talk session, especially before this afternoon."

"Okay dear heart, don't worry, all will be well, you'll do just fine. Come by the room when you're done."

"Thanks mama."

CHAPTER 2

"I thought you weren't coming by here until later son, what brings you by so early?"

"Good morning mother, I needed to talk to somebody and I figured I'd stop by and talk with the person who knows me the best."

After leaving Regina to finish packing for her trip, Bishop Montgomery drove around until he pulled up at his mother's house, Mother Betty Montgomery. At near eighty-four years old, she was still ticking with no real signs of slowing down any time soon.

Shuffling from the front door through the foyer, Eugene followed his mother through to the kitchen, she suggested, "Come on in and I'll make us some tea."

The two sat at the kitchen table.

Sensing something was wrong, Mother Montgomery asked, "So what's going on with you young man?"

Bishop sat back in his chair with one arm thrown over the back of it and said, "Where do I begin? How much time do you have?"

Mother Montgomery chuckled a little, "Oh I'm sure it's not that bad son."

Before he could start, the kettle whistled to them, alerting them it was time for tea. Only this time, he stopped his mother from getting up and he went to the stove and brought everything over to the table.

Settling down back into his chair, Bishop didn't waste any time, he asked, "You've always been a fan of Regina, can you tell me why she's now choosing to be gone when I need her the most? When our family and the ministry needs her too? I haven't been able to get through to her, it's like now, she's always gone. Have you talked to her lately?"

Mother Montgomery sipped her tea, "I make it a point to stay out of married folks business."

Bishop slammed his tea cup down and asked, "Since when?"

Mother Montgomery didn't answer, she continued drinking with a raised pinky.

"Mother, things are falling apart, all around me. Here I was looking forward to retiring and spending more time with Regina and now there's no way I can turn the church over to Carson after what he did and it looks like Regina isn't at all interested in retiring anything. Man, I can't believe Carson did that to Scarlett."

"Has anyone tried to reach out to her at all?"

"I've asked around and apparently no one knows where she is. It was hard for me to believe that she'd just leave him like that but Carson sold us all on the fact that she did. She obviously did what Carson told her to do which was to get lost. I don't blame her though. I can only imagine what that poor girl must be going through and thinks about us, we weren't there to help her."

Mother Montgomery interjected, "What about the other girl, anyone heard from her?"

"The last conversation Carson and I had he said he didn't know where she was either. This is all a big mess. How could I have not seen the signs? You know what Mother, I don't know how you and daddy did it. I guess I never really considered the other two. If I'm honest with myself, I viewed Carson's charisma over his character or even better yet, his competence to lead. Of all the boys, he was more charismatic. By him being the oldest, I just assumed he should've been the one to take over the leadership. I can't believe that boy, I get upset just thinking about what he did. Here I am thinking he's going to continue on and perpetuate the ministry, carry on the family legacy but based on things I'm now hearing about Carson, the only thing he was interested in was perpetuating himself. On top of everything he did, he's now sick, living with Leukemia in his body. What kind of leader am I? Real leaders leave behind true successors to take their place. Tell me mother, how did you all know I was to be the one to lead the church?"

Mother put her cup down and crossed her hands, "Son, you are a fine leader. I think you showed true leadership in dealing with Carson. Upon his admission, you rebuked him privately as well as openly by promptly sitting him down and relieving him of his duties. I'm sure it was hard to do but it was necessary."

Taking another sip of tea, she said, "Now your father did what he saw his father do and that man did what he saw his father do. All of them thought they were doing the right thing with respect to their appointments. At least, I know your father did. He thought by you being the oldest, you should have been the one to take over and I have to say you've done a fine job. Now, would your brother have done a better job, I don't know…he didn't stick around long enough after you were appointed. Once he realized he would not ascend to the throne, he left."

Mother Montgomery and her husband birthed four sons through their union, one died at birth, another died serving his country in the Vietnam War, and the other two, Carson Eugene and Claude Ebenezer Montgomery remained. Claude left the ministry shortly after his brother was given the church and started his own ministry in the next town. Despite being close in distance, the relationships were nonexistent, once Claude left, he built a huge emotional wall to separate him from his family.

"After all these years, do you ever think he'll come around?"

"Who knows, I pray for him all the time and I do pray that I get to see him once more before I make it out of here. It's a shame he took your appointment to heart like that, to keep himself away from us the way he did, even from me. The only way I get to see him now is on television through his church program. He feels like I loved you more than him, he made it very clear to all of us to leave him alone."

Trying to change the subject, "So, you have no thoughts on what's going on with Regina?"

Placing her hand over top of her son's she said, "Regina's my girl so hear me when I say, let her do what she feels she needs to, she needs to feel your support." Doing her own subject changing she asked, "So what else is going on? When is Cayden-James' appeal?"

Bishop's eyes squinted, "Next week."

"Are y'all going?"

"That's the plan but with everything going on in this family, who knows?"

Pouring another cup, Mother Montgomery said, "It's just praying time son, we can't stop. Did you know Christian stopped by to see me yesterday?"

"Oh yeah, did he tell you about all he and Courtney have been going through? I tell you, you talk about praying times, those two alone have been keeping me on my knees."

Mother Montgomery laughed, "I told him the same thing I told you that I don't get in the middle of married folks business but I had to laugh when he told me she filled his mouth with hot sauce while he was asleep because she was mad at him for reigning in her spending."

Bishop and Mother Montgomery could barely talk as they imagined the scenario, Bishop said, "Christian said he felt like a volcano had erupted in his mouth, he said he was on fire."

"The part that got me was he said, Grandma, how about the name of the sauce she used was Scorned Woman. He said, the heifer that made that sauce must've been real mad when she made that mess. But you and I both know, they over there feuding this week but will be all in love next week. I'm not paying either one of them any attention with all that foolishness they have going on over there."

Wiping tears from their eyes from laughing so hard, Bishop said, "I needed this, I'm glad I stopped by to see my favorite gal. Thanks for always having my back mother, if no one else does, I know you got me covered. I'm going to get going but I'll still stop by later to take you shopping."

Reaching in, Bishop kissed his mother on the cheek and gave her a hug, she squeezed him tightly and said, "Alright son, I'll see you later."

CHAPTER 3

"This is island living at its best huh? Have you been enjoying yourself this week Travis?"

"Yeah man, this has been great. I really appreciate you going out on a limb and inviting me along on a family trip."

"Oh don't think of it, we're family. I'm just glad you were able to come along. You know, don't take it too personal, I mean, Minta and Scarlett will come around. In a way, I think Minta may even be a little jealous. Poor girl, her father rejected her not once but twice. So, she didn't grow up knowing him and when she found him, he didn't want anything to do with her. Which is why I think she might resent the fact you found me and we're getting along so well. But how do you think things are going with them?"

Since Scarlett's baby shower, Travis hadn't had to work to insert himself into the personal lives of the Watsons because George was doing that all his own, almost force feeding everyone a big spoonful of Travis.

However, before Travis could answer his father, George looked up and shouted, "Hey there tiger, where are you storming off to?"

Jolted from his trance by his father-in-laws voice, walking without a mission, James was walking along a network of beautifully paved pathways strategically placed along the lush grounds of the resort. At the sound of George's voice, James stopped abruptly and turned to see George and Travis enjoying a late breakfast out by the pool.

"Hey son, c'mon over here and join us will you?"

In all honesty, James was not in the mood, in times like these, he'd much rather be left alone, but he put his hurt feelings aside and joined the men.

George offered James a playful elbow shove and jokingly said, "Are you already trying to give Scarlett the slip, are you trying to get away from her? I told you when you married her, I don't accept refunds, she's all yours now."

Travis and George laughed….James didn't.

"Cat got your tongue James?" George asked.

Shrugging his shoulders, James shook his head no, and then said, "I'm sorry y'all, my mind is all over the place right now."

Making a swaying dancing motion in concert with the towering coconut palms blowing in the wind, George closed his eyes and said, "How can you be thinking about anything other than sand and sun in a place like this?"

A bright-eyed Travis agreed with George, "I know right, this place is amazing."

James didn't necessarily have anything against Travis but knowing Scarlett was upset by having him on vacation he was now annoyed at his very presence, he scoffed at Travis' excitement.

Both Travis and George took notice.

Travis excused himself from the table.

Taking a more serious approach, George leaned in and asked, "You don't seem like yourself, what's going on with you?"

James and George had many things in common but the most important thing they shared was Scarlett. They both loved her very much and for that reason, James felt comfortable talking to George.

First taking a moment to apologize, James said, "I'm sorry George, I didn't mean to interrupt your breakfast and I'm sorry I'm in a jacked up mood. Scarlett said something that really cut deep with me, I can't seem to get it out of my head, it just keeps playing over and over again. I mean, I've done everything I know how to do to try and reassure her that we're going to be fine, that I'm not going to let anything happen to her and the baby but it's like she keeps drifting further and further away from me. I'm trying to be supportive and I was trying to be supportive when I agreed to take her back to that church but we should've never gone there. That's her past and it needs to stay there."

George asked, "So this trip hasn't helped any? It's such a beautiful island, I was glad when you told me about it, I figured it might do us all some good. I just hate it Cole and Marissa couldn't join us…maybe next time though."

"Oh yeah, that's part of the problem, Scarlett is not happy Travis is here, she said, she'd rather get to know him on her terms not have him shoved down her throat while she's on vacation."

Not lending any understanding, George said, "She wouldn't feel like that if Cole and Marissa were here, now would she? No, she would not. Whether they all like it or not, Travis is my son and he's not going anywhere so they may as well get used it. I mean, will they ever give the poor guy a break, all he wants is a chance. All he wants is a family. Now, I understand my daughter has been through a lot but she needs to keep her priorities in line and family is always a top priority."

Biting down on his bottom lip, James confided in George, "Man, can I be honest? I'm worried. I don't have to tell you because I hope you can see it but I love Scarlett. I'd do anything for her and Chandler. I mean, I love everything about her, even the things that drive me crazy, I still love them because those things make her who she is. When she walked into my life, I was walking around on autopilot, but then the more time I spent with her, I realized I wasn't dreaming anymore but wide awake.

Sounds starting sounding clearer, things started looking brighter, and I was able to actually feel again with her."

George chuckled a bit, "Boy, my daughter must've put it on you, you are all kinds of whipped."

James smiled slightly, "I mean George, I'm a surgeon for goodness sake; I deal with life and death situations on a daily basis so you know I can't let emotions have control over me. But when it comes to Scarlett, I just can't seem to control how I feel about her. Haven't you had that one woman that just messes you up completely?"

George laughed and said, "Uh yes and her name is Minta. Boy, how do you think I put up with Minta like I do? Listen, Minta is something else. As much as that woman drives me crazy, she has a hold over me like no other woman has. She sunk her claws in me a long time ago and I've been hooked ever since."

James wasn't in a joking mood but he was amused by George, he directed the conversation back to his situation, George, I'm worried this thing with Carson is going to be too much for us. I don't know what I'd do if he just tried to swoop in here and take Chandler or better yet, realize what he missed and tried to get Scarlett back."

George jumped in and slammed his hand on the table, "Oh no sir, that'll never happen. Not on my watch, oh no sir buddy…not happening."

Placing his hand across James' shoulder, George asked, "Hey, do you want me to talk to Scarlett?"

"No, not at all. I'm probably worrying too much; I just want everything to get back to normal."

Nodding his head, George said, "And I'm sure they will, just give her a little time. So, what time are your parents getting in? I can't wait to meet them."

Since the time he'd sat down, this was the first time James cracked a genuine smile, "Their flight is supposed to arrive at the airport around four and they'll take the speedboat over to the island like we did which will be about a twenty minute ride so I expect them here around four-thirty or five. They are so excited about meeting you guys as well and especially baby Chandler."

Getting serious again, George asked, "So, they are really alright with you marrying Scarlett and adopting my grandson?"

James threw his head back and said with a wide grin, "Oh yes, man they can't wait to meet those two. Plus, not only that, even if they weren't they'd have to live with it because as long as I have anything to do with it, those two aren't going anywhere any time soon."

"I hear you son, I hear you. Well, in that case, I'm looking forward to spending this weekend with them. I think I'm going to go check in on my Mrs. before she tries to give me the slip."

James finally laughed at George's joke, "Alright George, I'll catch up with you later at dinner."

CHAPTER 4

Arriving back in their villa, James was disappointed to see Scarlett was not there. He hadn't seen her since their argument that morning, he'd spent the day thinking and praying in a cabana on the beach. He was ready to see his wife before the welcome dinner for his parents. He figured, he'd settle with seeing her later because he needed to get ready to make sure everything was in order for the dinner.

He'd made special arrangements to host a family dinner on a nearby private island so that everyone could finally meet and get acquainted. When he told his parents about the trip and that George and Minta would join them to help with the baby, the Hartgrove's decided they wanted to come along as well even if they couldn't be there the entire time. James thought it was a great idea and figured the more the merrier.

By now, both Drs. Derrick and Rena Hartgrove had become professional laureates for the ground breaking work their research facility conducted. They would be receiving honors at a conference with a sizable cash award and would let the trip to Chee Chee Island serve as a celebration for their latest award as well as a reunion and meet up of their new daughter-in-law and grandchild.

Being on the island, James decided against shaving, he was enjoying crossing over to the dark side, but he was classy with it. His face accepted the stubbly hairs in sweet surrender to frame him as the epitome of a man who had it going on. Splashing the aftershave over his face the glass bottle slipped from his hand and poured into the sink. Although he was trying to concentrate on the evening ahead, he was still bothered by what Scarlett said and now he wouldn't have time to speak with her before the dinner.

Cleaning up the mess, he took one last look in the mirror, nodding and approving his island styled outfit featuring cream colored linen pants and matching vest and leather flip flops. The white shirt underneath, rolled up to his biceps showed off his fashionable muscles.

Grabbing his things he sat back on the bed, said a quick prayer, and left the villa.

On the other side of the resort, Scarlett was in her parent's room, stressing over what to wear to the dinner where she would be meeting her new in-laws. Minta and George paid her no attention as they continued getting themselves dressed and taking stolen minutes to play with Chandler who was ready for a night out with the family.

Checking the time on his watch, George yelled, "Scarlett girl, you have about five minutes before we need to be leaving, the boat is probably down there waiting for us now. I saw James earlier and he told me he was going to go ahead of us but that the boat would be here to pick us up."

A long, flowy floral maxi dress decorated Minta's body for the evening, Minta had been feeling better than ever these days. Her skin was tinted from the sun of the island, and it paired well with her dress, she radiated a healthy glow.

Making one last round around the villa and placing Chandler in his car seat, Minta said, "I don't think you should be late the first time you're set to meet his parents Scarlett. Whatever you don't have on now, don't worry about it. Come on and let's go."

Scarlett yelled from the other bedroom, "Alright, alright I'm coming."

Within seconds, a vision of beauty emerged, Scarlett walked out wearing an eggshell ruched empire styled dress with a neckline that highlighted her enhanced bust line. The openness of the back showed off her freckled back and the cap sleeves draped flawless over her shoulders with cascading ruffles.

George grabbed his chest, "You look beautiful sweetheart. Well, I guess looking like that, Chandler will be staying with us again tonight."

Scarlett blushed as she picked up Chandler's baby bag, she begged, "Please don't go there daddy and will you please try not to tell too many bad jokes tonight."

George cracked a smile and said, "I beg your pardon, none of my jokes are bad, everybody laughs at my jokes…isn't that right man?" George reached down and rubbed Chandler's cheeks and he replied with a smile to his grandfather. George said, "See what I mean Scarlett, I even have little babies smiling at me."

Scarlett laughed and said, "See that's your problem, you don't know when people are laughing at you and not with you."

They all walked out of the room laughing. At the boat docking station, Travis was already there waiting.

CHAPTER 5

"Mom, dad. How wonderful it is to see you guys, I'm so glad you could make it. Mom you look wonderful, Dad…you don't look too bad yourself."

Hopping off of the boat and onto the fine, white sand, the Hartgroves all greeted each other and walked over the dining area. As they walked, they got caught up on things. Derrick, James' father, reached over and placed his hand on his son's shoulder and said, "Boy, now that was real nice of you but you didn't have to order us that big 'ole basket."

Rena interjected as she kissed her son one more time, "The welcome basket was very thoughtful of you son." Getting right to the point, she asked, "Now, where is this new family we're supposed to be meeting? I'm ready to get my hands on that little Chandler, I'm ready to kiss those sweet little cheeks of his."

James led his parents to the candlelit table where they would be dining and said, "They shouldn't be too far behind, I asked you all to come a few minutes early so we could spend a little time together before they all got here."

Looking out over the horizon, James said, "Well, that sure was quick…I think this might be their boat."

Just as he thought, the other half of the dinner party, the Watson clan was cruising across the crystal blue waters.

James motioned for his parents to come join him at the water's edge so they could be there when the boat pulled up.

Shaking all over, Scarlett didn't know what to expect, she'd recently had a run in with one mother-in-law and was about to meet a new one, she battled with the thoughts raging in her mind as to whether or not the Hartgroves would approve of her and her baby.

Keeping her eyes on everything, Minta whispered a directive under her breath to her daughter, "Pull yourself together...now."

At Minta's last word, the boat stopped.

James quickly leaned in to help the women off of the boat and grabbed the baby.

Within minutes, salutations, hugs, introductions, and handshakes were being had by everyone.

Scarlett couldn't help but stare at her new in-laws, for people who'd chosen careers based on brains over brawn or beauty, both Rena and Derrick were stunning, they were one fine looking couple.

James pulled Scarlett close to him and spoke directly into her ear, "You look gorgeous." Being that close to James made Scarlett forget all about her previous apprehensions, he too, was looking gorgeous.

Once the introductions were all made, James grabbed Scarlett by the hand and led everyone to the beautifully decorated table. As everyone found their respective seats, James stood at the head of it and made an announcement, "Tonight is a very special night, two families are officially coming together, I'm so happy to have my parents here with us. I'd like to congratulate them on their most recent award. Congrats Mom and Dad."

The Watson family all smiled and clapped in honor of the Hartgroves latest achievements.

James continued to speak, "I've planned a few things for us tonight to celebrate family and there's one thing I want to do first before we get started."

Clearing his throat, James continued by looking directly into Scarlett's eyes, "Scarlett honey, will you come stand up here with me?"

Honoring her husband's request, Scarlett joined James up at the head of the table. He turned to face her and said, "Lately, I've been finding myself thinking about what my life would be like without you in it and the thought alone tears me up inside. I know that with what happened to you in your first marriage, somehow you became disillusioned by the possibilities of real love. You became suspicious of a true man's intentions but I want you to know in front of our family that I love you with all of my heart. I'm not that other guy, he messed around and let you go but he had to let you do so I could find you. My parents weren't around to see us get married and we didn't get to a have real wedding so tonight, I'd like to know if you'd like to marry me again?"

The tears streaming down her face could not soothe the burn in Scarlett's checks, through emotion filled words, she asked, "What are you talking about James? What is up with you always proposing marriage when you least expect it? Of course, I'll marry you again but where?"

Taking Scarlett by the hand he commanded everyone to follow them.

On the other side of the sand dune awaited the family, members from the resort who'd set up a beach side wedding ceremony. The candles, the chairs, the arch, the flowers, the entire setup was breathtaking.

Standing with her hand over her mouth, Scarlett couldn't believe what James had done.

Everyone took their seats and he led her to the spot where they would renew their vows and handed her a fresh cut bouquet.

Initially, James and Scarlett shared a commitment ceremony in her hospital room where Minta facilitated that one and days later when she was released, they went to the Justice of the Peace and were officially married. However, tonight, James knew he was sealing their fate and their future with this ceremony.

Under the moonlight and the stars, James and Scarlett pledged their love for one another in the presence of both their families for the third time within the last three months.

Leaning in to kiss his bride, James whispered to Scarlett, "I love you."

At the end of the ceremony, a steel drum band showed up playing melodies that got everyone excited as they walked back over to their dining area for a champagne and lobster reception.

The celebration was underway and the festivities were in full swing. Clanking his glass, Derrick Hartgrove stood up and shouted, "Toast, toast, I have a toast. Torquato Tasso once said, true love cannot be found where it does not exist, nor can it be denied where it does. Judging by what I've seen here tonight, I can safely say true love is present here, there's no denying that. Congratulations to my son and my new daughter, Scarlett."

Glasses were raised with all on one accord and they said, "Cheers."

The team from the resort started the five course dinner menu, James had picked out for the evening. Over the course of dinner, memories were being made. Old stories were being told, James' parents were sharing about him and Minta and George had stories to share about Scarlett.

Knowing full well the evening wasn't about him, Travis couldn't help but think, "They both have their families here to talk about their childhoods and upbringings but I don't have anyone to recall stories about me."

He sat quietly and listened to the chatter around the table.

Listening to the Hartgroves speak, Scarlett was in awe. She knew James was smart but seeing him interact with his parents, she was realized how highly intelligent he was. With a permanent smile plastered on her face, Scarlett sat watching James thinking, *"This man really does love me and I need to stop making him pay for what another man did."*

Flipping the conversation around onto his parents, James started talking about what it was like to grow up in a household with scientists.

Getting Minta and George's attention he said, "You guys do realize scientists speak to their children differently, right?"

George sat up and said, "How so James, do tell."

James said, "Well George, I'll start out by saying I'm going to offer you a constellation of perspectives on the matter. That is word for word what my parents said to us when my siblings and I wanted to pick out a restaurant."

The table erupted in laughter, Derrick and Rena being the ring leaders, hearing these stories now provided them with great enjoyment.

James kept going, "Hold on, wait a minute. I'm sure you never told Cole and Scarlett, I'll pick you up from school around two o'clock plus or minus ten minutes, did you?"

George and Minta looked at each other and said, "Nah, can't say we ever used that one."

The Hartgroves were too tickled.

Offering more stories, James said, "Most people would expect science to be glamorous but when you are people like Rena and Derrick, you're like nerd celebrities, these two are rock star scientists, so you can imagine growing up in that kind of pressure. I used to hate people asking what I was going to be when I grew up because I knew answering anything contrary to the Hartgrove dynasty would draw stares."

Rena spoke up and said, "But you've grown up to be a wonderful and loving man, just like your father and look at you, you are a great doctor."

James smiled at his mother and then at Scarlett.

Derrick jumped in the conversation and said, "I guess you know, in building our careers, we never considered the impact our careers would have upon our children but obviously it did."

Rena added over top of what Derrick said and offered, "Which is why we were shocked when James called and told us he'd become a born again Christian a few years ago."

Minta turned their way and asked, "And why were you so shocked?"

Rena explained, "We were shocked because in our field, it is our job to prove things to be either true or false. We base our entire theories upon hypotheses and when you talk about a God or Jesus like he's real when he's actually something you can't see, touch, or hear, it makes us believe that it is one big fairytale. We raised our children in something more tangible, in the universal goodwill towards all men."

Tapping her foot under the table with a pinched expression, Minta asked, "Can you see a molecule?"

George placed his hand over Minta's in an effort to speak through body language by saying, *"Don't start."*

Poking out his chest, Derrick titled his head back while Rena winked and offered Minta an easy nod with flair by saying, "Why yes, that's part of the reason we were honored. Our state-of-the-art research facility was the first ever to photographically document atomic bonds and how their molecular structures change in a before and after state."

Things had been going wonderfully but James could see this particular conversation had the potential to have long-lasting impressions. While the final course was being served James took back control over the conversation and said, "Well, that's why I told my parents, that contrary to what they believe, Jesus hears, sees, and touches me every day and that's proof enough for me."

Derrick looked at James and said, "I have nothing but love for you son and I highly respect your beliefs."

Catching the eye of one of the resort team members, James knew it was time, he asked everyone to join him for another surprise.

The group moved from their table back out to the shoreline and waited for further instructions from James. Before he could say anything they heard a loud, BOOM...BOOM...BOOM, followed by a spray of sparkling colors in the sky. Up above their heads was a fireworks display for them to enjoy.

Scarlett pulled James off to the side and kissed and hugged him. Looking deeply into his eyes she confessed, "You are such an amazing man and I don't know what I've done to deserve you. Truth is, I have been making things a little difficult between us because of what has happened and the potential of what could happen. But I promise, I'm going to try and not focus on all of that stuff and concentrate on you...on us. I love you James and I appreciate you for putting up with me."

James held Scarlett close, looking at her and then their family along the shore line, from the looks on everyone's faces, he felt confident he'd pulled off a fantastic evening for the family.

CHAPTER 6

Turning his phone towards Marissa, Cole said, "Ah man, will you look at that? Scarlett just sent me some pictures, looks like she and James had some sort of ceremony on the beach."

"Oh how romantic, Scarlett looks beautiful, as she always does." Marissa replied.

"With these final exams calling, it was too bad we couldn't be there but we'll get to see them at my graduation next week."

Marissa pressed her lips together before stating the obvious, "We aren't going to be able to keep this from them much longer, you do realize that don't you?"

Cole stood up and walked into the kitchen, walking away, he said, "I'm not trying to keep anything from them, we just haven't had the right time to tell them. There is a difference. My family has been through a lot here lately and I didn't want our news to be overshadowed by all of this other drama, you know what I mean right?"

Starting then stopping, Marissa started her sentence by saying, "Yeah but I'm worried as to how your mother is going to react. Nothing seems to get by her and I think she's the type to get upset by not being one the firsts to know…anything."

Sitting down, Cole kissed Marissa on the cheek, "You are kind of right, she can be a little spit fire when she wants to be and she is kind of nosey but I promise you it's all out of love, my mother does mean well. You two seemed to get along at Scarlett's baby shower, right?"

"Yeah we did, she was very nice to me and quite hospitable despite the shock of my presence."

"I'm sorry baby, that was my fault and you know as well as I do, I was going to make it right and tell everyone that weekend but then my dad had to go and drop that big brother bomb on us. Geesh, I still can't believe it."

Marissa inquired, "Have you talked to the guy at all? Are you trying to get to know him?"

Cole drifted off in thought for a minute, then he answered, "You know what, I always wanted a brother. Growing up with Scarlett was fine but she was older and a girl so we didn't have much in common so I always wished I had someone around to share guy things with. My dad was great doing those things but I just wanted someone around my own age to hang out with. Now that I have one, I'm not sure what to think of it. More than anything I don't like the way he stepped to my mother and the way it all came out. We all were having a great time until that happened….but to answer your question, no, I haven't spoken with him."

"Cole, are you going to at least give him a chance to be your brother?"

"Who knows, according to Scarlett, my dad is trying too hard to get us to like him but I guess, I'll see for myself when they come here next week for graduation. If my dad treated him to Chee Chee Island, I know he'll be coming here."

"Well Cole, if I can weigh in, I think you should give the guy a chance. He might not turn out to be half bad once you get to know him. He is part of the family and George seems to be making every effort to bring him into the fold."

Marissa rubbed Cole's head, "Give him a chance sweetheart. I'm going in the room to study for a while and then I'm going to bed."

Cole looked up and smiled at Marissa, "Okay baby, I'm going to finish studying out here and then I'll come to bed. I need to get my rest, my last college final is tomorrow morning at eight o'clock, so don't be trying no hanky panky stuff tonight."

Marissa walked down the hall smiling saying, "Whatever."

CHAPTER 7

"State your name and number soldier."

"Cayden-James Montgomery, number 309729."

The officer unlocked Cayden-James' cell and said, "That's you, now come on."

Asking questions, Cayden-James wondered, "I just got back here, did they forget something."

Not divulging any in-depth details, the officer said, "All I know is you have a visitor."

Cayden-James sat down to a table where he'd sat earlier. He'd been in a meeting with his attorneys about his upcoming appeal and he figured they must've forgotten to share some information with him.

The door opened but it wasn't a member from his team, on the surface, the woman walking to him seemed unfamiliar but deep down, something connected him to her. Closely watching her walk to the table, he wondered, *"Who is this woman and why is she her to see me?"*

Ali Joyner sat down in front of Cayden-James and for a moment they both sat in silence and examined one another.

Unable to bear the silence, Cayden-James decided to break it, "Hi, excuse me but …do I know you?"

Ali ignored Cayden-James' request for more information. Focused on the moment at hand she sat still and looked him over once more, taking in the moment of being able to finally sit across from him.

The intense, fevered stare she gave made Cayden-James feel like a deer in lights, the high-beam ones. He couldn't figure out what was going on, trying one more time, he said, "Can I help you with something? Otherwise, I'm getting ready to go back to my cell."

With flaring nostrils, Ali said, "Happy to go back to your cell now because you know you're about to get out soon?"

Turning away to gather his thoughts, thoughts that were swirling around in his head, he said, "Huh? Who are you and how do you know I could be getting out soon."

Ali began to slowly reveal the nature of her visit, "Yes, I finally saved up enough money to make it here to sit in front of the man who killed my father."

Cayden-James' mouth opened but nothing came out, he couldn't believe what she'd said. When he could finally speak, he said, "I'm sorry but I think you have the wrong person. I didn't kill your father ma'am."

"No buddy you are the right person. You ruined my life and my family and I hate you for that. You killed my father and now you're more than likely going to get released from here next week and go on about your happy little life."

"I don't know what you think you know about me but you know nothing about my life and for the last time I didn't kill your father."

"Well you may as well had. You tell me what do you call it when your father loses all his money in a financial scam. Money he'd saved up to send me to college with. He worked hard so I wouldn't have to. He never got a chance to go to college but wanted to afford me the opportunity to do so. He transferred his money into bitcoins and started trading them to make up the shortfall for my education. Lo and behold, he gets hooked up with your bitcoin bank and loses everything. I couldn't continue on with school because even with financial aid, I still couldn't afford to keep going. The thought of me not finishing school hurt him to his heart. So much so, he died from a heart attack."

Wanting to appear smaller or better yet, disappear, Cayden-James offered his condolence and said, "I'm sorry for your loss but I paid restitution to all of my victims and I've apologized to each and every one of them."

"Yeah but my dad died before he got the money back. With your case being so high profile, it took time to get everything all sorted out."

"Well again, I'm sorry for your loss. Whether, I get out of here or not, I've taken responsibility for my actions and I've repaid my debts. Yes, my choices hurt a lot of people and I've let a lot of people down but I promise I'm doing what it takes to make positive changes in my life. But get this, even after your dad died, you got the money so why didn't you get back in school?"

"With my dad being gone, my mom needed the money, plus you know after the government got their piece with all of the taxes, we didn't get nearly the amount close to his initial investment."

In an effort to be respectful and show interest in Ali's misfortune, Cayden-James asked, "What were you going to school for?"

A slow building smile escaped from her frowned mouth, as she spoke, her face brightened a little, "Psychology, I'd like to help people figure out why they behave the way they do."

Cayden-James offered, "Well, you'd have a job in my family once you're done because we need a lot of figuring out."

Realizing she was laughing and not seething mad anymore, put Ali in an uncomfortable position. She was to be there to avenge if only for a minute the death of her father based on the events surrounding Cayden-James' greed. However, he was more inviting than she'd expected, his delightful and thoughtful conversation was in direct conflict to how she thought she'd spend her time with him.

The guard announced, "Five more minutes and your time is up."

Looking up at the clock, Ali let out a sigh, she had not had a chance to unload all of the rants she'd practiced over and over in her head. She hadn't had a chance to tell him what an awful person he was or a disgrace to the American dream. Tilting her head down and frowning, she accepted the fact she'd never get to tell him to go to hell for all he'd done. The time had been too short and now it was about to be over and if things went the way she thought, he'd be leaving there within a few short days.

Living in his head, trying to figure out how to end the awkward yet pleasant meeting, he lost touch with what was happening around him, before he had time to consider what he was saying, he blurted out before leaving, "Tell me, tell me quick, what's your number?"

Before she could offer him an expletive or a directive such as for him to go for a long walk on a short pier, Cayden-James got up to leave and Ali spoke up, "555-321-1097."

CHAPTER 8

Living with leukemia for the last several weeks felt like an eternity and Carson wasn't making it easy on anyone to care for him. Suffering from a rare type of leukemia, his body was producing an overgrowth of immature blood cells and the mature blood cells weren't replenishing fast enough. While this was taking place on the inside of his body his condition of immaturity seemed to carry out into his personal life. He refused hospital stays, opting for home care and within six weeks, he'd already been through seven nurses.

During the initial weeks after the diagnosis, he'd been given a lot of literature but didn't want to educate himself on his condition.

Since his confession in front of the congregation at Wondrous Works, he'd lost all track of time, the days all seemed to roll together. Unwilling to keep track of dates, he was unaware of how long it had been since he'd heard from Rebekkah or even Scarlett for that matter. He figured, she'd truly left him as Scarlett had supposedly done.

From his first round of chemotherapy, his once wavy locks was now being thinned out by the radiation. His facial hair was unkempt and scruffy. He was mostly weak as chemotherapy treatments intentionally reduces the immune system. Most days he stayed in bed, paranoid at the sounds of a settling house. The shadows of nurses throughout his home freaked him out, so much so, he made anyone entering his home wear either bells or chimes around their neck while present.

Checking the time, he realized his morning nurse, Karen wouldn't be there for another hour, he sat up in bed and turned on the television, it was still dark out.

Flipping through the channels, he couldn't find anything to watch but his channel surfing was cut short when he heard a noise at the front door.

Being upstairs didn't quiet the noise, his persistent fear made him sensitive to any and everything going on in the house whether it was happening for real or mainly in his head. The first attempt to unlock the front door was unsuccessful but minutes later the front door opened.

Waiting to see if he'd hear bells chiming, after a few minutes went by and he didn't hear them, he thought, *"Who is this in my house?"*

With each footstep that made it closer and closer to his bedroom, he called out, "Who's there? Karen is that you? Where are your bells?"

The shadows on the walls kept coming closer.

No one responded.

Being the type of man he was, he may have been sick but he wasn't going to let someone take him out in his house, reaching for his newly delivered hand gun, he tiptoed to the corner of his doorway. Not aiming at a particular target, he stretched out his hands, fired, and shot.

Shots rang out in the hallway, and he immediately heard screams and shouts of, "Oh my God, I've been shot. Oh Lord, I'm going to die. Jesus Christ of Nazareth, help me. You idiot, I can't believe you shot me."

Expecting to hear the voice of an intruder, he ran into the hallway when the familiar voice registered to him.

Kneeling down to the ground, a screaming Rebekkah was lying on the floor squealing and withering in pain, "I'll never forgive you for this Carson. Is this what we've been reduced to, you just go around shooting people these days?"

Frozen in the spot where he was, feeling rooted there, Carson was staring but not seeing his wife before him. His mind had completely shutoff to what had just happened. He trembled and stuttered with tremors in his voice, "What are you doing here? Why didn't you answer me when I called out who was here?"

"Dude, what's up with all these questions? Do you want me to die lying here or are you ever going to call 9-1-1?"

Pulling himself up from the floor, Carson grabbed his phone and called for emergency assistance. He also placed a call to his father.

Within minutes, fire and rescue along with law enforcement arrived with Bishop pulling up right behind them.

The technicians attended to Rebekkah and determined she'd need to be flown to the nearest hospital for surgery.

Bishop spoke with the responding officers and based on his position, they agreed to sort things out and take statements later in the day.

In the beginning, each of the Montgomerys dealt with the news Carson's illness in different ways. For some, initially it was very hard but during this time, he and his father, Bishop Montgomery had become closer as a result of his illness.

Bishop Montgomery picked out some clothes for Carson and waited for him to get dressed so they could go to the hospital with Rebekkah and to the police station.

Bishop prayed this news wouldn't get out, he knew ministry couldn't afford another bad publicity story right now after Carson's recent scandal. He thought to himself, "*Another incident involving Carson, Lord help us.*" He did all he could to prevent the spread of the shooting.

Getting inside the car, Bishop said, "I've made a few calls trying to get ahead of this thing but boy, you have some explaining to do. Are you trying to self-destruct? Or are you trying to take down the church since you didn't get it? How on earth did you get to the place of shooting that woman?"

Trying to plead his case, Carson shook his head, with his hands flapping in the air, "Bishop listen. You've got to listen to me. It all happened so fast. Essentially, she broke into the house. I haven't seen or heard from her since the night she left. I had no idea she would be coming to my house. Since she's been gone, I've even changed the locks so I'm not even sure how she got in."

Bishop scoffed, "Man, Carson…you're too predictable, everyone knows you leave spare keys under the flowerpot, she probably got the new key from there."

Resting his head back on the head rest, he continued to explain, "I called out asking who was there but she didn't answer. What was I to do, let someone break into my house and kill me? I might be sick but I still know how to defend myself."

"Defend yourself from your estranged wife huh?"

With his hands over his eyes, Carson acknowledged, "My life is really jacked up. I'm thinking I must've been a really bad person in my former life."

Bishop quickly pointed out, "Not just in your former life son, try this present one. And tell me this, since when did you become a card toting member of the N.R.A and get a gun?"

"I just got it last week. Hey, uh does mother know yet?"

Letting out a huge sigh, Bishop responded, "Last week huh? No, I tried calling her but she didn't answer."

Staring out of the window, Carson said, "Are you freaking kidding me. Someone please tell me I'm dreaming. Like, did I seriously just shoot my wife? With everything going on around me can things get any worse?"

CHAPTER 9

The late night wedding celebration didn't stop the family from getting up bright and early for sun and a whole lot of fun.

After a quick bite of breakfast, the crew was ready for a day filled with exciting water adventures. Waiting for their boat, the chatter from everyone was building the enthusiasm and anticipation amongst the group.

Once settled on the boat, George picked up his phone and starting snapping selfies with everyone. Covering her face with her hair, Scarlett begged, "Daddy…please."

Not paying any attention to Scarlett, George continued, "Girl, these pictures are going on my Instagram."

In sheer terror, Scarlett yelled, "You have an Instagram account…Lord help us all." Looking at her mother, Scarlett asked, "Did you know about this madness?"

Minta giggled, "Yes, I have one too."

Intrigued by the conversation, Derrick and Rena asked, "What is it? Maybe we should get us one?"

Scarlett swung her head back in response to her in-laws and said, "Oh not you two."

Minta stepped up and offered, "Here you guys, hand me your phones. Apparently our daughter seems to think we're too old to be up on social media but I happen to have profiles on all of the sites."

Everyone was laughing, including Travis when they were interrupted by the boater's first announcement, "We've made it out far enough for anyone that would like to drop a line and do a little fishing. We're going to hang out in the spot for a while to see if you catch anything, feel free to jump in the water and go for a swim. Let's have some fun."

George didn't wait, he was the first to dive into the ocean for a swim in the beautiful waters. He beckoned for the others, "C'mon you guys, jump on in."

Travis and James followed suit while the ladies stayed on board.

Watching the guys, Rena struck up a conversation with Minta, "So Minta, I understand you are close to retiring."

Nodding her head, Minta acknowledged her, "Yes ma'am. I'm turning my practice over to the next generation of consultants."

With a smirk, Rena asked, "So tell me, how does one become a church consultant?"

Raising a perfectly arched eyebrow, Minta answered Rena's question with a question, "How does one become a scientist?"

Hopping back on the boat, George dropped a fishing line into the water and hopped back in the water.

Overhearing the mother's conversation between Minta and Rena, Scarlett did not want to be in the middle of where that discussion was headed so she removed her cover up, exposing her new motherly figure in her one piece and followed her dad into the water.

The guys all cheered for her flawless dive into the water, in high school, Scarlett had been on the dive team. She was good enough to land a full ride to college on a diving scholarship. Being a proud husband, James pulled her close and said, "You still got it baby."

On the boat, Rena and Minta were left with a sleeping
Chandler who was outfitted in the cutest pair of swim shorts and
sun hat.

Choked up by Minta's response, Rena said, "Uh I mean, you
know…I grew up taking things apart, I always wanted to know
how things worked, so I'd start at the end and work my way
backwards to the beginning. I knew I was destined to be a scientist
from a young girl, it was just something in the cards for me. So
what about you?"

In no uncertain terms, Minta was often intolerant of those
unlearned about her profession and most importantly the church.
Therefore, Rena's comment about not believing in God had Minta
feeling unsure about establishing a real relationship with her
despite her having raised a wonderful son in James.

Minta replied, "I was born and raised in the church and that's
all I've done my whole life is go to church so I've seen a lot of
things. I went to school to become a nurse but every time I visited
a church, I always felt like I had something that could make them
better. I felt like I had a prescription for making the church
healthier, better to serve the needs of the congregation. I didn't
want to be one of those ones who talk about the problems but not
be willing to offer any solutions. So I decided to do something
about it. First, I prayed and I waited for the Lord's leading and
then I searched through a lot of scriptures on how the early church
was formed and with my background in nursing, I began to put a
plan together. I started with my local church and then when results
started showing up, other churches started hearing about what was
happening and they started calling me and the rest is as they say,
history."

Repositioning her wide brimmed sun hat, Rena inquired with a small giggle, "What's all in involved with waiting for the Lord? I've never heard of such a thing in my life."

Minta's virtuous tones were clothed in smugness, her smile appeared to be forced, "Because the Lord speaks to me, I waited to hear an answer from Him. He's always speaking to us, we just need to be willing to listen."

While Rena claimed to not believe, she was somewhat intrigued by Minta and her conversation.

The group broke up their exchange when they all climbed back inside the boat to grab some refreshments.

Just as George was drying off, his fishing line became taut, he had a catch. Running to his pole, he motioned for Travis to come over and help him. As he ran to the pole, he tossed his phone to Scarlett and said, "Here, take some pictures of me with my phone."

The line was too strong for Travis and George, James ran over and tried to help, with three strong armed men, the catch was still too strong. Man versus nature was taking place before everyone's eyes and nature was winning. In a round of apparent tug of war, standing on the sidelines, Derrick jumped into the mix and the men pulled with all of their might. The slippery deck caused Derrick to lose his footing, he slipped and fell backwards as the other three continued to fight against the weight of George's catch. Jumping back up to help, with one last pull from all of them, the promise of a beautiful bounty was emerging from the water. Scarlett switched from taking pictures to capturing video as Minta and Rena cheered from the sideline.

Finally seeing what was snagged on George's line, everyone shouted with excitement, the boat captain led them to the onboard scale. Everyone's eyes feasted upon a twelve hundred pound blue fin tuna as George stood smiling from ear to ear.

After such a tremendous experience, the boat captain offered to serve the family lunch before the next activity.

During the lunch hour, there was no shortage of conversation, everyone was talking and getting to know one another better. The topic of conversation migrated to everyone's top ten favorite movies and Minta looked over at Travis and said, "What are your top ten Travis?" All before now, she had been trying to be alright with him but she hadn't had much conversation for him so he threw his head back in amazement when she questioned him. Responding quickly he said, "Oh yes ma'am, that's easy, The Godfather – all three parts, Gladiator, Star Trek, Coming to America, Star Wars, Transformers, A Soldier's Story, Carlito's Way, A Time to Kill, and Forty-Two."

Everyone nodding their heads, Minta replied, "That's an interesting list you have there Travis." Listening to him speak about his favorite movies, she realized, she had not been the nicest and that she needed to do better to include him in their lives. For it didn't appear he was going anywhere any time soon, especially if George had anything to do with it.

Finishing up lunch, everyone prepared for the next activity which had been chosen with Travis in mind because he'd never gone water skiing. Their boat captain set everything up and George and Travis got ready to lead the pack, they would be the first two to begin. Because George was going to go with him, Travis opted out of the basics for beginners the boat captain was trying to offer him. He was just anxious to get outfitted with his skis and life jacket.

Down in the water, as they both held onto the tow, George looked over at Travis and asked, "You ready son?"

With a huge smile, Travis yelled out, "Yeah baby, let's do this."

Minta said under her breath, "He doesn't have a clue what he's doing."

Rena overheard her and snickered.

The boat captain counted down, five, four, three two, one...and the boat started moving again.

George glided through the water for about a minute and then steadied himself onto the water. Travis on the other hand, wasn't ready yet, he quickly thought, "*Maybe all those videos I watched on YouTube didn't teach me how to do this. What am I supposed to do next, they are all looking at me; I need to do something.*"

With shaky knees, Travis hoisted himself on the skis and on top of the water. George offered him a thumbs up of approval.

As they slowly coasted along on the water, George gave the signal to increase the speed of the boat.

In getting a hang of being on the skis, Travis thought, "*Oh this isn't so bad; I can do this.*" He decided to entertain the family by doing some tricks by letting go with one hand to wave at them. He was doing fine until the boat hit a small bump in the water and Travis lost complete control of his surroundings, he fell backwards with the tow still in his hands and ended up being hauled by the boat. George was yelling, "Stop, stop, stop the boat." However, unable to hear from the water, the boat continued until Minta ran to the front of the boat to alert the boat captain to stop.

Once back on the boat, with her nursing knowledge coupled with motherly intuition, Minta examined Travis. He was all bruised and bloody and it appeared his leg had been broken as well. It was clear to everyone their day on the water had come to a disastrous close.

Back on dry land, the medics were waiting on them to arrive. Travis was so grateful Minta looked after him on the boat that he took her hand and said as he was being transferred to the gurney, "Thank you so much for looking after me and everything is okay now. You don't have to worry about me and be jealous of me anymore, I know how your father treated you but you and George accepting me is the best thing that could've happened to me."

George's neck bent forward, openly staring at Travis, thinking, *"That boy must've really bumped his head out there on that water, why would he talk to Minta about her dad, didn't he know that was a private conversation between the two of us?"*

As the gurney pushed past Minta and George and George said, "We'll see you at the hospital Travis."

Baring down on her teeth, with cold, flinty eyes, Minta deepened her tone as she stomped off saying, "GEORGE."

CHAPTER 10

A quick jolt back to reality was what Rebekkah felt as her anesthesia wore off and she awakened to find her arm bandaged and in a sling.

Using one hand to reposition herself she looked over and threw her head back saying, "Jesus, what are you doing here?"

Seated in the corner looking like a member of the hazmat team, Carson scooted over to the bed and said, "I'm here to see about you."

Trying to find him through all of his garb, she said, "If you have to go through all of this why even bother?"

With a weakened immune system, the slightest cold symptom could set him back so being in the hospital with Rebekkah, Carson couldn't take any chances, yet he steadily contended, "I'm here to see about you Rebekkah. I mean, the police were here earlier interviewing me and they said they'd be back to question you but for goodness sakes, what were you doing at my house this morning?"

Rebekkah rolled her eyes and said, "The last time I checked, I thought it was still our house."

Carson scoffed, "I owned that house before you and you gave up the our house part when you left me. Remember that? Speaking of, where have you been anyway?"

Glancing around uneasily and choosing to respond slowly, Rebekkah answered, "Technically, I'm still your wife so I share in some part of that house and I've been around."

"If you feel like that, why did you chose to come back today? What was it about today that made you decide to show up? If you're still my wife as you put it, where has my wife been and why is she all of a sudden showing up unannounced?"

Rebekkah interjected, "I tried calling you."

"Well, I had to change my number. And not being able to get me wasn't an invitation for you to come by, you should have tried to reach me before you came by. Not only that, you didn't answer when I asked who was in my house. I haven't seen or heard from you in over a month, you would have to know that even under better circumstances I'd be shocked to see you. You left me right after my diagnosis and I'm still living with it so I had no reason to believe I'd ever see you again."

Going on the offensive, Rebekkah began to verbally attack Carson, "You know what Carson, that's the problem with people like you, always blaming other people for your mess. You can't seem to take a look in the mirror because you're too busy looking out the window. And I guess it's my fault you shot me. Please, give me a break; I see you're still a piece of work. And to answer your question, I'm still gone, I only came back to the house to grab more of my things."

Carson stated an obvious fact, "In your letter, you said I'd be hearing from your attorney but that hasn't happened yet. Is there any particular reason you haven't served me with divorce papers?"

Rebekkah sneered at her husband, "And you still will; I meant it when I said I was done with you and this sham of a marriage. You don't want a wife, you just want someone you can control and baby, I'm here to tell you that I'm not the one."

Carson spoke softly, "You used to be the one. What happened to Team Carson?"

Shaking her head slightly and upset with the limited mobility of her arm, she grimaced at the pain, "I don't think you get it. I seriously don't think you get how awful of a person you are to live with and I just couldn't put up with your foolishness anymore."

For most of her life, Rebekkah questioned being left handed but it served her well that day, she'd been shot in the right arm, so she didn't have to worry about not being able to use her dominant arm but the pain was still annoying nonetheless.

Feeling comfortable enough, Carson decided to probe into a suspicion he had, "I bet Godfrey filled your head up with all of this talk about me, didn't he? We all found it funny that both of you disappeared around the same time. Now that you're here, maybe he'll pop back up too."

Wagging her finger and berating Carson for his accusations, she fired off at him, "See what I mean, this hasn't nothing to do with Godfrey but everything to do with you and your inability to take responsibility for your own actions. You need to grow up Carson."

Carson took in what she said and then filtered out a follow up question, "So I guess that means no about Godfrey?"

Incensed at his same old ways, Rebekkah was about to sound off on him again when she was interrupted by the attending doctor, a gentle yet firm female doctor, Dr. Roberts.

Taking a seat by Rebekkah's bed, Dr. Roberts looked over at Carson before she spoke a word of Rebekkah's condition, he spoke up and said, "Hi, I'm her husband."

Smiling, Dr. Roberts asked Rebekkah how she was feeling and to try and quantify her pain level to see if more medication was required. Rebekkah made a face, she was indeed in pain, she reported, "If I had to guess, I'd say my pain level right now is about a nine."

Dr. Roberts reviewed Rebekkah's chart before speaking, "Well, I hate to hear you're in pain but that's to be expected, you do realize a fiery piece of metal pierced through your arm and tore your flesh where we had to go in and remove all that we could."

Carson winced at Dr. Robert's description.

The doctor continued, "While I will provide you with some pain medication, we're going to have to be careful for the you know, for the sake of the baby."

Finding it difficult to articulate a simple question, Rebekkah slowly asked, "Huh, what baby?"

Dr. Roberts looked at both Rebekkah and Carson and said, "Oh, you didn't know? Well, in that case, I guess congratulations are in order. Looks like you two are going to be having a baby. When you came in we did a complete body scan on you and from there it was determined you are expecting."

Stumbling over her words, Rebekkah asked, "Pregnant? How far along am I Dr. Roberts? Did the scan show that?"

"According to the scan, you are about ten weeks along. I've been waiting for you to wake up so I could check on you but it seems like you may need some time. I'll be back to check on you later."

Unsure of what to think, Carson sat up against the wall thought to himself, *"She's pregnant? Is she really now just finding this out? Ten weeks huh? I knew there wasn't anything wrong with my little swimmers."*

Dr. Roberts wasn't out of the door fast enough before Carson scooped in to take control of the conversation, "A baby? You and I are going to have a baby? Am I finally getting ready to get my son? This is wonderful news, how do you feel about this Rebekkah?"

Shock and surprise were two words that could describe Rebekkah but the occasion seemed to need much stronger words to accurately define how she was feeling. Resting her head on her pillow, she looked over at Carson and said, "I'm not sure how to feel right now. I can tell you what, this is not how I'd plan to spend my day today."

With a glimmer of hope in his eyes, Carson leaned in and said, "So, you know you have to come back home now."

Snapping back, Rebekkah said, "Oh no I don't. This doesn't change anything for me Carson."

Taking off his facial mask, Carson looked directly at Rebekkah and said, "It should because it changes everything for me. You know how long I've been waiting to have a baby and now you're the one who's going to give me one. For the first time in weeks, I feel like I now have a reason to live and get better. Hey listen, I'm not asking anything from you until we sort all of this out but I need to be a part of this pregnancy with you and since I'm unable to get around much these days, it makes sense for you to come back home…we could both have nurses to rehabilitate us. It could be like real life couples therapy." Pleased with himself, Carson smiled while Rebekkah remained quiet.

Unable to think straight, Rebekkah's mind had shut off which turned into a problem once the authorities came to interview her.

Carson excused himself and assured her, with a generous smile that he'd return soon. He may have been sick but he still possessed a winning smile and the news of a baby made him beam with pride.

CHAPTER 11

"What on earth were you thinking telling that boy my personal business?"

From the moment the words rolled out of Travis' mouth, he knew he was in big trouble with his wife.

Stripping out of her clothes from the boat trip she yelled out, "For the life of me, I don't understand what kind of hold this boy has over you that you do things without thinking."

Standing with his hands on his waist, George said, "What kind of hold? There is no hold Minta, he's my son and he's trying to be a part of the family. Now, I was probably wrong for telling him that without your permission but c'mon is it really that big of a deal?"

Raised by a single mother, Minta grew up without a father, she actually grew up not even knowing who he was until she was a senior in High School. When a handsome, young suitor, Morris Thatcher, came knocking on her mother's door asking to take Minta to the Prom, her mother, Harriet Woodson responded as if she'd seen someone familiar with devastating consequences. Instinctively, she knew upon sight. As a result, the young man wasn't allowed in the home and Minta was left without an explanation and most importantly, no date to the Prom.

How could Harriet tell her daughter that the young man was wanting to become her boyfriend was indeed her half-brother?

Morris' father, Jacob Caldwell was a traveling minister but he had a problem, while he was married with six children, he enjoyed the company of young women, young enough to be his daughters. One of those young women happened to be Harriet and when she became pregnant, he distanced himself and stopped coming to that particular area. He warned her that if she told anyone he'd deny her accusations and that people around town would shun her. He convinced her that it was best for her to go on without him and that's what Harriet did.

As a teenager, Morris' mother, Maggie Thatcher, turned out to be one of Caldwell's victims as well and bore a son with him, Morris. She too had been given the same speech and just as Harriet had done, she raised Morris without his help.

Known to eavesdrop, Minta wanted answers, no, she felt like she deserved them. Overhearing a conversation between her mother and Maggie, Minta heard her father's name for the first time in her life.

Growing up, she longed for the days of knowing his name and what he looked like or what he did for a living. She dreamed of the days he'd show up to take her out for an afternoon or tell her she was beautiful. There were times she'd envision laughing and talking with him and enjoying his company as a dad. Unfortunately, those days never appeared and they were never going to.

Inquisitive by nature, Minta probed further and knew what needed to be done next. Without her mother's knowledge or permission, Minta tracked Jacob Caldwell down. At that time, he was now in a state of advanced age and despite being in his golden years, he still wasn't ready to accept his struggles and the impact those said struggles had on others, including his illegitimate children.

Turning his back towards Minta, Jacob profusely denied the accusations, calling Minta all sorts of names outside of the God given one her mother had chosen for her.

The real life abandonment she experienced from him penetrated deeper than the imagined and perceived rejection she'd felt all of her life.

In his moment of denial to his youngest daughter, an invisible hard veneer finish coated Minta as she walked away from her biological father.

Walking back and forth up the hallway with her hands up, Minta yelled, "You know what the big deal is George about my father and you share that information with Travis…I can't believe you."

George remained calm, "Listen, you look like you were starting to give Travis a chance, so don't stop now because of this. He didn't do anything wrong, I did and I apologize. In an odd sort of way, I think he was on some level trying to connect with you using that story. Nevertheless, I'm going to head over to see him at the hospital shortly and I'd like for you to go with me."

Minta scoffed, "There you go taking up for him again."

George's calm demeanor was now starting to become forced, "Hey, listen, seriously, can I ask you something? How much time and energy have you already invested in being mad about Travis and this whole entire situation? I mean, when you think about it, could you have been doing something else more positive with that time Minta? You have got to let up and stop holding onto all of this negativity. Time is too precious for us to be being upset about things we have no control over. Honey, all I want is for us to be happy and enjoy life. Can we just do that…please?"

Feeling numb, Minta refused to respond to her husband's questions and his request. She crossed her arms and turned walking down the hallway without saying a word.

CHAPTER 12

Praying for an easy going day, Regina declined lunch with the host pastors in an effort to pray and meditate before her evening speaking engagement. She'd been ignoring the calls from home, she figured she'd return calls after the service.

Concentrating on the task ahead, Regina stared out of the backseat window on the way to the church.

Standing at the side door, the host pastors were waiting to greet Regina as the car pulled up, the Co-Pastor Joyce Fulton was the first to step up and embrace her, "Hello there First Lady Montgomery, it is a pleasure to have you with us for tonight's service. C'mon in."

Pastor David Fulton followed suit, he leaned in and said, "Welcome sister, so glad to have you here."

Joyce turned around and led Regina into her office, she revealed a display of some of Regina's favorite things, "So I have your hot tea, honey, and lemon all ready for you. When you are ready, we can get you fitted with a lapel mic and if you'd like to take a look for inspection, the product table with some of the merchandise from Wondrous Works is set up for you in the main lobby with two of our best people to work it for you. Also, the items you requested are on the stage for you."

Offering praise to the Fulton's, Regina said, "Everything looks wonderful, I appreciate all of the warm hospitality so I'm sure the table is well represented."

Checking the time, Joyce said, "We have about twenty minutes before service, we're going to leave you now and we'll see you out in the sanctuary. You can let Armia here know if you need anything, she'll be right outside this door."

One of Regina's conditions before speaking included a twenty minute session alone with the Lord, no one was to interrupt her during that time and as she sipped on her tea, the countdown started.

With five minutes left, she equipped herself with the microphone and waited for the knock at the door.

Right on time, Armia knocked and opened the door for Regina, she led her to the front of the church where she was seated next to the Fultons.

For a Saturday night, the service was well attended. Joyce Fulton was hosting her annual Women's conference and Regina was the Saturday evening guest speaker. Women flocked to the church for a chance to hear Regina Montgomery speak. The word was spreading as to how she was preaching a brand new message and people were responding well to it. Everywhere she now went people weren't showing up for her name recognition but they were showing up to hear about the name she was preaching about and that was the name of Jesus.

One more song of worship and she'd be up, she was centered and prepared. Regina was ready to let the words of her mouth and the meditation of her heart be acceptable in His sight, she was ready to complete her assignment.

Joyce rendered a beautiful introduction and welcomed Regina onto the platform, the crowd stood and applauded. As Regina took control of the stage, she pointed at herself and wagged her finger back and forth shaking her head no and then pointed up above indicating the praise belonged to God. The claps and cheers grew louder from the flock as they understood who was to be glorified.

Regina began with all of the normal and expected pleasantries thanking the Fultons and acknowledging everyone in their respective places.

Not wasting much time, she opened her bible and said, "We are all at different stages in our walk and this maybe a familiar message to some and to others this may be your first time hearing it but nevertheless, whether you're a veteran or a virgin, listen up because this is something we all need to hear. Will you look at your neighbor and say, sometimes you just need to be reminded."

Regina had a gift for pulling people in, she knew how to hook them and keep them reeled in for more until the very end. The group followed her instructions and repeated her words, she continued on, "Now, our base scriptures for tonight will be coming from Matthew 25:14-23[1]. As I said earlier, some of you may have heard of this before but because we all are still here, here on earth, we all should be striving to hear those precious words, well done good and faithful servant. It's a little quiet in here tonight, I hope I'm not the only one wanting to hear those words on the Day of Judgment."

The assembled group perked up somewhat by acknowledging they too want to hear those words.

---

[1] **Matthew 25:14-23: 14** For the kingdom of heaven is as a man travelling into a far country, who called his own servants, and delivered unto them his goods. **15** And unto one he gave five talents, to another two, and to another one; to every man according to his several ability; and straightway took his journey. **16** Then he that had received the five talents went and traded with the same, and made them other five talents. **17** And likewise he that had received two, he also gained other two. **18** But he that had received one went and digged in the earth, and hid his lord's money. **19** After a long time the lord of those servants cometh, and reckoneth with them. **20** And so he that had received five talents came and brought other five talents, saying, Lord, thou deliveredst unto me five talents: behold, I have gained beside them five talents more. **21** His lord said unto him, Well done, thou good and faithful servant: thou hast been faithful over a few things, I will make thee ruler over many things: enter thou into the joy of thy lord. **22** He also that had received two talents came and said, Lord, thou deliveredst unto me two talents: behold, I have gained two other talents beside them. **23** His lord said unto him, Well done, good and faithful servant; thou hast been faithful over a few things, I will make thee ruler over many things: enter thou into the joy of thy lord. (**KJV**)

Regina began to set the foundation for her message, "In this passage of scripture and actually in this entire book, we see that Jesus was a masterful storyteller. When He spoke, He used illustrations and stories in His teachings, often times, His style of communication when He taught was through the use of parables. An understanding of parables is essential to understanding the teaching of Jesus because they have Kingdom implications. It has been estimated that parables make up approximately 35 percent of His recorded sayings. At no point are the vitality, relevance, and appropriateness of His teaching so clear as they are in his parables. Which says to me that we need to have some conversations about these parables. The way He taught was not just to offer up some bedtime stories but these stories were intended to stimulate thought. In case you were wondering, Jesus did not spoon-feed His hearers; rather, He taught in such a way as to bring about a response, and where there was a response, He gave additional teaching. Consequently, it is not merely satisfactory that parables are interesting, poetic, and arresting but parables are to also stimulate thought and bring about response. Based on what I'm about to say, before we leave here, I want for us to all have a response tonight. Amen."

Everyone responded, "Amen."

Flipping through the pages of her bible, Regina said, "In talking about the parables, remember when I said the parables have Kingdom implications? I think it's important to note that Jesus' teachings are like an indication as to how we are to make ourselves ready for life eternal in God's Kingdom by illustrating to us how to live correctly here on earth while we're still here. Now, parallel to Matthew, where we have three servants, there's another story in Luke 19 with ten servants and while there are some differences in these two stories, there are some similarities that I'd like to focus on. If this is supposed to be a lesson for us as to how to live in this life and prepare for eternity, I think in order for us to understand what's going on here, I think we should start at the base level and determine what it means to be a servant. The basic term "servant" has many meanings. It is used some eight hundred times in the Old Testament, and can mean a slave, an officer close to the king, or to the chosen leader of God's people. The New Testament variously defines servant as a hired servant or hireling. I believe if you're a born again believer, I believe 1 Corinthians 7:23 explains it nicely for us, we've been bought with the precious blood of Jesus and should now consider ourselves servants to Christ[2]. 1 Corinthians 6:20 states again that we've been bought, we no longer belong to ourselves. Hey, I don't know about you all but I couldn't think of a better master, what do you all think?"

Those in agreement nodded, some shouted, "Yes," while others agreed by saying, "Amen."

Finding her stride, Regina went for it, "In Matthew 25, we see Jesus is comparing the Kingdom of heaven like a man leaving on a trip. This particular man calls over his servants, these servants were believed to be three of the most trusted. In the King James Version, it states each servant received talents in accordance with their respective abilities. Therefore, one man received five talents, to another, he received two talents, and the third one, received one. While they each received different amounts, two of the servants did the same thing. Now, I want to ask you a question. Do you think these three servants struggled with the weight of having received something from their master? Do you think they struggled with what to do with that in which they had in their hands, whether to be obedient or not? Keep in mind these were trusted servants. Sometimes, when God gives us an instruction or

---

[2] **1 Corinthians 7:23**: You were bought with a price [purchased with a preciousness and paid for by Christ]; then do not yield yourselves up to become [in your own estimation] slaves to men [but consider yourselves slaves to Christ]. (**AMP**)

places something in our hands to do, it may be hard, we may struggle with it but we must be like the first two servants if we are ever going to make a difference in this world. And what did they do you ask? Well, the bible says that both, the one with the five and the one with the two went at once and traded them. However, the one who received the one went and dug a hole in the ground and buried his master's money. Now everyone look up here at me."

Regina asked for three volunteers to reenact the scene, to one she passed out five gold coins, to another, she presented two coins, and to the other, she handed out one. Knowing the story, two of them went off and pretended to do something, while the third pretended to dig a hole with the shovel on the stage.

Turning towards the audience, Regina asked, "How do you think you'd feel if you were the master and you came back to this situation?"

Returning to the servants as the master, Regina walked up to them to settle up their accounts…to judge them. The one with the five talents came and brought her five more, realizing he'd been entrusted with five and had proof for the gains on his investment. The same thing happened with the one with the two talents, he'd doubled the initial investment. Both servants received praise and a commendation, as the master, Regina turned to the servants and said, "Well done, good and faithful servant, you have been faithful over a few things, I will make you ruler over many things: enter into the joy of the Lord."

Looking out to the crowd, Regina said, "Those two were faithful with what they had been given. While we can speculate as to whether or not they struggled in the beginning, the point is that they allowed their faith to take over and they immediately went off and did something with what they'd been given. As a result, on the day their accounts were to be settled, they had no shame, no fear, they brought evidence of their service to their master and they were rewarded. Now that other one, tsk tsk, if he was struggling with what to do, he should have looked at what his fellow servants was doing but instead, he chose to do nothing. Consequently, instead of receiving a reward he received a quick lesson in God's mathematical process. Notice if you will, the other two brought forth their increase but the only thing the grave digger came forward with was a bunch of excuses about how he was afraid. Isn't this how some of us do, when we don't have anything to show, we make up reasons."

The nods clued Regina in that she was at least making sense to a few people.

Finishing the rebuke, she said, "The first two were called good and faithful, while the third one was called wicked, lazy, and idle."

Walking up to the third servant, she spoke as the master, "If you were so afraid, you should have at least put my money in the bank instead of in the ground, I mean, that way I could have at least gotten some interest."

Standing in front of the lone servant, she took away the one talent and gave it to the one who had the most and said, "Those who have much will receive more and will have more than they need. However, for those who don't have much, even the little bit you have will be taken away. So since you decided to play-it-safe and not go out on a limb for me so you shall be thrown into utter and complete darkness."

Regina thanked all of the volunteers and walked back to the podium, saying, "Let's give the guys a hand. Now I mentioned Luke nineteen and very quickly I want to point out that two of the ten immediately went away and did something with what they had been given whereas the third one tucked it away for safekeeping then when he was called out, he had an excuse. Turn to your neighbor and say, no more excuses."

People were saying no more excuses as Regina prepared to close, "Each and every one of us has been given something by God to do and listen here, we need to get to work doing whatever it is. Whether you believe it or not, a time is coming where our accounts are going to be settled. I would pay attention to the admonishment in Revelation 22:12, behold, I am coming soon, and I shall bring My wages *and* rewards with Me, to repay *and* render to each one just what his own actions *and* his own work merit. I believe we're closer to His return more than ever before. He's soon to come y'all, for He came to seek and to save that which was lost and as his servants, we share in that same service. The way we invest and use what we've been given is to get to work and share His story of redemption so that everyone can have an opportunity to share in His victory. In the top part of Matthew twenty-five, the story about the ten virgins was to point out to us to be watchful, to not get caught sleeping when He returns and here with the servants, we're learning how to get rewarded for when that day does happen. It's time to get to work church and it's not about what and how much you've been given but it is all about being faithful with what you have been entrusted with. If we can learn anything from these three parables mentioned tonight, I'd say be ready, be faithful, be serving. We need to live in a sense of readiness. Are you a good steward over the things God has given you? I want you to consider that as I close. I think Galatians 6:4 sums it up nicely and I particularly like it in the message bible translation. It's time out

---

[3] **Galatians 6:4-5**: "Make a careful exploration of who you are and the work you have been given, and then sink yourself into that. Don't be impressed with yourself. Don't compare yourself with others. Each of you must take responsibility for doing the creative best you can with your own life." (**MSG**)

for looking at what other people have and what you think you don't have and just do what God has placed in your heart to do."[3]

Closing her bible and her notes, Regina said, "Remember when I said, I wanted for all of us to leave with a response? Well, here it is. I want you to close your eyes for a moment and think about what would it take for you to finish well? What do you need to do in order to ensure on the day your account is up to be settled that you hear Him say, "Well done good and faithful servant, enter into the joy of the Lord? What is your response to that tonight?"

Regina's question turned into an appeal, for that moment, people came down to the altar for prayer and to begin the journey towards their response. To God be the glory, Regina had delivered another power-packed message filled with love and conviction.

After the service, Joyce hugged Regina tightly saying, "Woman of God, you blessed our hearts in here tonight. I think we sometimes get comfortable and actually end up plateauing in our walk but we are to continue in the faith and occupy until He comes. First Lady Regina, during the service, I found out that my morning speaker is dealing with a family emergency and will not be here in the morning. I would love for you to continue this message you've started here tonight, do you think you could stay and speak in the morning?"

Not giving any thought to her other obligations, she figured it would be better to ask for forgiveness rather than permission. Regina quickly answered, "Yes, it would be my honor and privilege to share God's word with His people on tomorrow. I'll just let my husband know, I'll be home a little later than expected."

CHAPTER 13

Tucked away in his office at the church, Bishop checked and rechecked the time. After the conversation with his mother, he'd actually begun to give consideration to the work Regina was doing, he'd streamed the service and watched her minister at the conference. His heart swelled as he saw his better half, the best half of himself, walk in her anointing and be used as a servant of the Lord. Yes, he was proud of her but he also knew it was about time for her to be calling to check in, there was much he had to share.

Minutes later, his phone rang.

"Hi honey. I know I missed you earlier but honey it's so nice to finally get to hear your voice."

"Hello Regina. I want to see you, we should do a video call instead."

Dialing Regina through his computer, Bishop decided a phone call wasn't enough, if he could be next to her at least he could lay eyes on his wife.

At the point of the connection, he immediately said, "There's my beautiful and gorgeous wife."

Titling her head slightly she said, "Oh lord, what's gotten into you? You're being quite complimentary tonight."

"So a man can't complement his wife anymore, is there a crime against that these days?"

"No honey, I'm just teasing you."

Wondering if he should bring up that he'd watched the service Bishop sat quietly for a minute.

Unsure of his silence, Regina said, "I said I was only teasing, you didn't have to get all quiet on me over there."

"I'm here sweetheart, I'm just missing you is all. You know, I'll be glad when you get here in the morning, maybe we can squeeze in a little alone time before church…huh, huh?"

Regina blushed, "Eugene, listen at you. I'll be home soon enough and there will be plenty of time for that."

"So is that your way of saying no about our time before service?"

Pausing for a minute and lowering her head, Regina looked up on one side and said, "Yeah, about that." Rushing all of her words together in an effort to get out the news, Regina said quickly, "I won't be home until tomorrow afternoon, I've been asked to speak again in the morning."

Looking closely at the screen Bishop said, "You want to run that by me again. You're what?"

Using a slower tempo, Regina repeated her previous announcement.

Bishop's muscles jumped under his skin, "Regina, when is this going to stop? I mean, I can't keep living like this. Too much is going on and I need you here. Do you know why I was calling you today? Carson shot Rebekkah this morning."

Regina's mouth flew open as her hand flew to her chest yelling, "What? How did that happen? Is he alright? Is she alright? Where has she been all this time?"

With his pulse speeding and his heartbeat pounding, he said, "See, see…if you were here you wouldn't have all of these questions now would you. If you were here you'd know the answers to all of these questions. You'd know that I've spent the better part of my day trying to keep this out of the news. If you were here, you'd see how I've been trying to keep another son from going to jail and preparing to hopefully go and get our other son out of prison. If you were here, you'd know that I've had to try and save our other son from the prison he's currently living in which is his home with his brand new wife. Those two are really having problems.

Regina retorted, "Those two will be just fine, what they are going through isn't uncommon. They are just experiencing growing pains. The bible says the act of two becoming one is a great mystery. Honey, all marriages have problems."

Bishop scoffed, "Tell me about it. Ours is going through some very serious ones right now. Are we experiencing growing pains as well Regina?"

Not stepping down Regina said, "We've been through this before, I'm here for the family where it counts. Me speaking tomorrow morning isn't going to slow down anything going on back home. When I get back, we'll take care of everything together. Maybe in between putting out these fires we can sneak in a little alone time, isn't that how you put it?"

Unamused, Bishop's face went slack and he broke eye contact with Regina, he was no longer interested in talking with her any longer. He was tired of the song and dance she gave, all in the name of ministry when he felt like her first ministry should have been her home.

Offering a heavy sigh and a bitter smile, he said, "Alright, I guess I'll see you whenever you get here tomorrow. I know you'll do what you feel like you need to do. By the way, you did great tonight. Good bye Regina."

Not giving her a chance to respond, he clicked off the video call, he was completely over the madness that had now come between them.

Sitting in her hotel room staring at a blank screen, Regina sat there thinking, "*How did he know how I did, did he watch me online?*"

For a moment, she smiled, she was happy he'd tuned in, she realized, with time, he'd understand and eventually come around. Lightly touching the dark computer screen, catching a glimpse of her reflection, under her breath she mouthed, "I love you too honey." She figured by him mentioning the webcast that was his way of showing her he was supporting her and loved her.

The hour was growing late and she needed to prepare for the next service, her problems with her husband and his insecurities would have to wait. She opened her bible and began to sing the song, "*I'm going on.*"

CHAPTER 14

"Great service today Bishop."

Seated around the family dinner table, there were several empty seats. Carson was at the hospital with Rebekkah and Regina's seat, the one to the right of Bishop's was also empty. Mother Montgomery, Christian, and Courtney participated in the customary after church dinner.

Placing a forkful of mashed potatoes dripping with gravy and cheesy macaroni and cheese in his mouth, Bishop nodded his head in gratitude towards Christian.

The starchy combination was a part of Bishop's ultimate favorite meal, they were his ideal comfort food, he'd made a special request of Clarice to make those dishes along a hearty three meat, meatloaf. Despite the long day he had the day before and the unpleasant conversation with Regina he was still able to study for the morning message Christian was referring to, entitled, "And Suddenly."

Courtney blurted out, "Lord knows I'm looking for my and suddenly to happen. I'm ready for God to do something surprisingly with me. Thanks for the encouraging word Bishop."

Rolling his eyes, Christian didn't respond and continued eating.

Taking notice of the young couple, peering over the top of her glasses, Mother Montgomery added, "Courtney dear, you do realize life is full of surprises? You sit here saying you're looking for God to do a surprise in your life but never have I seen where we get to pick the surprise or pick how God chooses to do what He does. Everyday all day, all over the world, things are happening that we never would have expected. With one surprise, a person's life can change just like that so honey, be careful what you ask for because you may not always like what life may bring you. The important thing is to keep the faith through whatever is brought your way. You understand?"

Feeling a flush of redness through her cheeks, Courtney sipped a glass of water and simply said, "Yes ma'am."

In the short time Courtney and Christian had been married, instead of enjoying being newlyweds they were turning into warheads. Their new home was now a battle zone. No one ever came over to visit. They were constantly arguing and at each other's throats sometimes literally. Interestingly enough, their pattern of hostility towards one another fueled unbridled passion between the two of them. In a weird way, they seemed to be enjoying their new way of becoming one flesh. Either one or the other would purposely create a situation for the other to blow a fuse that would wreak havoc in the relationship, they now began breaking up just to make up because the reuniting now seemed to feel so good.

In an effort to change the subject, Christian asked, "Grandma, will you be traveling with us to Cayden-James's appeal on Tuesday?"

Mother Montgomery shook her head and said, "No son, I'm going to stay here on my post and pray. I know with you on his team, you guys are doing everything you can to bring him home."

Winking, he gave his grandmother an easy nod saying, "Yes ma'am, we are. I feel real good about this. Who knows, if he gets out, this maybe just what I need to get me that job I've been eyeballing."

Nearly spitting out her water, Courtney asked, "What job? I haven't heard you mention anything about a job?"

With a gleam in his eye, Christian said, "Yeah, I didn't want to speak to soon about it but yes, I'm being considered for a fantastic position at a high profile law firm. They recently lost their founding partner and they are looking for a few experienced associates to come aboard and provide some leadership

Passing on dessert, Bishop stood to excuse himself, "Hey guys, I'm not feeling so well right now, I think I'm going to go lie down for a while. Maybe I can get a little rest before Regina gets home." Initially, the requested comfort food seemed like a good idea but it didn't seem to provide him with the level of comfort he usually got from eating it.

Munching on a slice of Clarice's infamous pecan pie, Christian said, "That's not like him to pass up on Clarice's pie, I hope he's alright. I guess after yesterday, I can't blame him for wanting to take a little time to himself. I still can't believe Carson shot Rebekkah."

The two remaining at the table, Courtney and Mother Montgomery chuckled under their breath, knowing in their heart it was wrong to laugh but they just couldn't resist when hearing the words, Carson shot Rebekkah.

With a twinge of mischief, Mother Montgomery giggled and said, "I always knew something was off about him, that boy has always been a loose cannon."

Courtney and Christian couldn't contain the laughter this time, all three laughed at Mother Montgomery.

Christian looked at Courtney and said, "You two used to talk regularly before she left, had you spoken with her after she left?"

Leaning back, Courtney answered, "No, I haven't spoken to her since the day we left for our wedding. I tried calling her but she never answered my calls or text messages.

As only a lawyer could do, Christian tilted his head while weighing evidence and said, "I wonder what made her come back? I mean, I heard the story about her coming back for her clothes or whatever but c'mon, she couldn't buy more clothes. It's not like Carson cut her off, even after she left, she was still spending money. He's so whipped by her that she could probably take everything from him and he wouldn't care."

Courtney jumped in and said, "You think so? Now don't get me wrong, she does have his nose wide open but he doesn't strike me as the type to get taken by a woman like that."

Pointing his finger at both his wife and his grandmother, Christian said, "Yeah well we'll see what happens but I'm probably right just like I was about Scarlett. Y'all didn't want to believe me when I said there was more to the story but as it turns out, I was right all along."

Courtney's neck bent forward as she said, "I still can't believe that one and I was sitting right there watching him confess. Do either of you ever wonder where Scarlett is or if she's okay after what he did to her?"

Mother Montgomery chimed in, "As far as what I've been told, she did exactly as he suggested and started over because since his confession, no one has been able to find her. I was talking to Regina about it and she put her hand over mine with tears in her eyes and said, "In my heart, I know she's fine, our girl Scarlett is just fine. I didn't ask anything beyond that so prayerfully, Regina's conviction is true and Scarlett is okay, wherever she is."

CHAPTER 15

"Sweetheart, are you alright? The porcelain gods have been holding you hostage all night, do you need me to get you anything?"

Yelling from inside of the bathroom, Scarlett answered, from the bathroom floor, "No, I'll be out in a minute."

It was hard to determine which end would need the sparkling white bowl so Scarlett just rested on the floor in between rounds.

Slowly walking to the bed where James was seated on the edge, she said, "I think I have food poisoning."

Helping to get her back in bed, James did a spot check over his wife, he said, "You think it was something from dinner last night? Let me check around to everyone and see if anyone is sick."

James placed a call to his parents as well as to George and Minta, none of them were ill.

When George and Minta came back from visiting Travis at the hospital, the family went out to dinner at the resort. Scarlett was the only one feeling effects from the dinner.

James tucked her in and kissed her on the forehead, "I'm sorry you're not feeling well sweetheart. This is our last day here on the island and I had something planned just for the two of us. Since you aren't feeling well today that just means you and I will have to come back here again…alone."

Offering up a weak smile, Scarlett kissed James and said, "I agree."

James walked over to the table and said, "I just got a text from George, it looks like Travis will be able to leave with us tomorrow. They're going to release him in the morning before we leave."

Raising one eyebrow, Scarlett said softly, "Good for him, Travis gets to come home with us tomorrow. Hearing that news makes me feel like going back into the bathroom again."

James laughed, "Scarlett, you can't be serious. He looks like he's going to be around so you may want to start trying to get used to that. Do you think you can at least give the guy a chance?"

Before he could get an answer, Scarlett was already asleep.

Leaving Scarlett to rest, James picked out his last pair of swim trunks and grabbed a pair for Chandler. He figured he'd pick him up from George and Minta's and see if his parent's would like to spend some time together down by the pool.

Stopping by his parent's villa, he placed a call to Minta, "Good morning again, do you think you can get Chandler ready for me? I'm about to come down and get him."

Minta said, "Sure James, since Scarlett is sick, what are you two going to get into? Do you need me to come along?"

James shook his head, "No, I think we'll be fine. I'll be there in a few minutes."

Rena overheard the conversation and said, "Let me guess, she wanted to come along? Did it ever occur to her that we might want to spend some quality time with the baby? She acts like he belongs to her."

James kissed his mother on the cheek and said, "Mom, don't start. You just need to get to know her. In a way, you two are a lot alike."

Derrick laughed while Rena said, "I beg your pardon. Oh, I'm nothing like that woman."

Derrick chuckled and said, "Oh, I think you're exactly like that woman. You two could be sisters."

In a huff, Rena said, "That's simply impossible so stop saying things like that. There's no way she and I are sisters and we have nothing in common."

James smiled sweetly, "You have me in common. You have Scarlett and you both have Chandler in common. You are just as much his grandmother as she is."

A wrinkling forehead was an internal indication to Rena's uncertainty, "I guess you're right but I guess I won't really feel that way until we actually share a grandchild."

James rubbed the back of his neck and asked questions of his mother to elicit more information from her, "What do you mean until y'all actually share a grandchild? You do already, my son…Chandler."

Feeling trapped, Rena tried to smooth things over, "I know honey, I was just saying…"

James jumped in before she could finish her thought, "You were just saying what, that you've forgotten that I'm not actually Derrick's son. Apparently the years have clogged your memory that another man raised me and not my biological father." Pointing at Derrick, he said, "This man here, remember him, he took you in and made an honest woman out of you when that other guy abandoned you, left you…with a child…me. Do you realize by you saying that, you can't wait to actually have your own grandchild that you make me wonder if Grandma Hartgrove felt the same way about me. Did she not see me as an actual grandchild?"

Derrick interrupted, "It made no difference to my mother, she loved you from the moment she laid eyes on you. To her, you were her grandson, no question about it."

Tears rolled down Rena's face, she cut her weeping eyes at her husband and said, "Thanks Derrick for making me feel even worse."

He quickly responded, "Excuse me, you did this to yourself. You are the one still holding on, James and I have no issues between us. There's never been nor will there ever be a thing as bio dad or step dad, it's just father and son…he's my son and that's that. I admire him for doing the same thing with Chandler, that's what real men do. Our son is in love and I think he's found a remarkable young woman to share his life with. I don't think I could've pick out a better match for him and I couldn't be more happy for them. Rena, can't you see, it's like you and me all over again."

Pulling James in for a hug, Rena explained, "Yes, I do and don't get me wrong, I think Scarlett is a wonderful young lady, I like her, I really do but I guess I just got carried away and let my feelings get in the way. I'm sorry James and please know that I do love little Chandler."

Looking up at the clock she said, "Oh wow, you've been here for a while, do you think she has him ready now?" Gathering her pool bag, she said, "Would you like for us to meet you down by the pool son?" Glancing at Derrick, she said, "Grab your towel honey and I'll put it here in my bag.

James turned to walk out and said, "Change of plans. I'm going to get my son and he and I will be spending the day together; I'll see you guys later….maybe at dinner."

Slamming the door behind him, Rena broke down and started crying.

CHAPTER 16

"Hey, I'll be right back, I'm going to go check on Bishop."

Courtney and Christian started a movie after dinner but Christian couldn't focus because he was concerned about his father. Things seemed to be off with him and not having Regina home yet seemed to make things worse.

Walking towards the stairwell, the family dog, Barkli started barking alerting Christian to the presence of guests. Stopping at the bottom step, Christian could see through the window, sergeant styled hats walking to the front door. He knew instantly this could not be good news.

Opening the door, standing with the male and female officers, Christian recognized a friend of his father's, Chaplain Prather standing with them. Chaplain Plather spoke up and asked, "Uh, hello there Christian, is your father here?"

With each passing second, Christian's heart began to pound louder and louder, the strain in the chaplain's face made it worse, he gathered himself long enough to say, "Yeah, I'll go and get him. C'mon on in."

Christian's feet felt like bricks as he walked up the stairs to his father's room, his breathing was heavy and his body began to tremble. His shaky hands knocked on his father's door and he walked in to see a knocked out Bishop fast asleep.

Christian called out to him, "Dad. Dad…wake up. Dad, you need to wake up."

Even in a groggy haze, Bishop knew something was wrong because none of his children ever called him dad, the look on Christian's face confirmed what he was feeling on the inside.

Christian said, "There are some people here to see you, there are two officers and Chaplain Plather is here as well."

Quickly freshening himself up Bishop and Christian walked downstairs. Extending his hand for his dear old friend, Bishop said, "Hey there Brent, to what do I owe the pleasure."

The two officers stepped forward and said, "Is there somewhere we can sit down and talk?"

Bishop led the chaplain and the officers into the living room, Christian sat next to his father and the female officer cleared her throat, speaking slowly and carefully, she identified herself and her colleagues and stated their credentials. Short and to the point, officer Matthews said, "Bishop Montgomery, there's been an accident. There is currently an investigation going on but from what we can tell, the accident has claimed the lives of your wife, Regina Montgomery and your driver, Norris McDonald."

Norris had been a longstanding driver for the Montgomery family, he'd been there for over twenty-five years. He and his family were set to celebrate his granddaughter's first birthday, a big party was planned for early afternoon. After Regina's arrival time was delayed due to the extra service, Norris would now be late to the grand celebration. Within miles of the Montgomery estate, he was happy to being close to dropping her off so he could get home. Only he made a terrible mistake that cost him not only his life but also that of his longtime employer, Regina Montgomery. Texting a message to his wife, he wrote, "**Be home soon. Don't start the party w/o me. I love u.**"

Just as he hit the period key, he'd unknowingly crossed lanes and hit the guard rail causing the car to crash and erupt in flames. They both died instantly.

As the officers were delivering this news to the Montgomerys another death notification team was on the other side of town, meeting with the McDonald family amongst all of the party decorations.

A slow building screech that reached its crescendo emanated from Christian as he crouched down on the floor with his hands by his ears. His violent outburst and piercing cry drew Courtney and Mother Montgomery into the living room.

Despite having attended many of these types of visits, Chaplain Prather was burdened by this particular visit, he knew that telling someone that a loved one has lost their life is probably the worst possible news a person could receive but this time, it was personal. Noticing that Bishop Montgomery had not moved since hearing the news, he sat next to him. Bishop Montgomery stood up quickly and said, "Are you sure it was my wife and driver? I mean, I just read a story last week were the police went and told a family their son had been killed in a crash and it turns out it wasn't their son. Could this be the case here? Could we be dealing with a case of misidentification?"

Courtney and Mother Montgomery stood in the doorway and listened as Bishop belted out his questions, searching for answers. Courtney could stand there no longer, she ran to Christian where he was screaming inaudible words.

Chaplain Prather stood up, his voice trembled as he said, "Bishop, listen to me. I know this is hard to hear right now and a lot to take in but it's her. They ran the plates, the car belongs to Wondrous Works and they were able to retrieve some of her belongings where they found her driver's license. Now at some point, you will have the option to make a positive identification but from everything we know. I'm sorry but Regina's dead."

The weight of the news of Regina's passing caused Mother Montgomery to fall up against the cabinet in the hallway as she clutched her chest, her breath became short as she was suffering from a reaction brought on by traumatic shock. Her beloved Regina was dead, she was the daughter she never had and to accept she would not be returning home to them was more than overwhelming, it was debilitating. The officers had to carry her to a downstairs bedroom.

The news began to travel quickly through the house to the staff on duty, the most impacted, was Clarice. She was not only an employee but she and Regina had become close friends over her many years of service. They'd seen each other through some rough times in life and for Clarice, this was one of those times.

Still standing in the middle of the floor with his hand on his waist, Bishop Montgomery was still trying to make sense out of what he'd been told. The news seemed to have caused his brain to contort because he couldn't make it understand how Regina was now dead when she was supposed to be on her way home. It just didn't make sense.

As the tears were flowing with the immediate family, the officers and the chaplain knew there would be a need for immediate support and compassion. The scene in the home was highly emotional. Out of respect for the family and in an effort to treat the bereaved family with the utmost dignity, they offered to hang around for a while to answer questions or assist in any way.

Going into preservation mode, Bishop snapped his fingers and said, "There's only a matter of time before this news gets out so I need to call Carson and Cayden-James before they hear it from someone else. I guess I need to call Mrs. McDonald as well."

Speaking loudly, Christian demanded to know, "What are you going to call her for, because of her husband's negligence he killed my mother, your wife."

Chaplain Prather stepped in, touching his arm saying, "C'mon on now Christian."

Yanking his arm back, he yelled, "Get your hands off of me man."

Bishop started to explain but he thought better of it, he turned and walked away. Searching for his phone, Bishop walked around the house looking for the small device. Upon finding it, he picked it up to call Carson but before he could do that he saw a message from Regina, it read: **"Destiny has been fulfilled again 2day and I'm on my way home honey. Thx 4 ur support and I love you."**

Reading the message, for the first time, he felt his emotions trying to connect with what he was feeling on the inside but he wouldn't let it, he looked at the message once again and then threw the phone up against the wall, cracking it as it crumbled to the floor. He took the same path as the phone, down to the ground.

Clarice ran to comfort him.

Not by much but Christian was in a slightly better state and said, "I'll call Cayden-James, he should probably hear this from me anyway. You guys can decide who will call Carson."

Courtney stepped up and said, "I'll call Carson and then I'm going to call my parents and then I'll go in and check on Grandma Montgomery."

Christian grabbed her arm with bloodshot eyes and a raspy voice saying, "Thanks Court."

Shakira R. Thompson

CHAPTER 17

"What time is Travis supposed to be arriving? I hope we don't miss our flight because of him," Scarlett said trying to put something light on her stomach.

George updated their group, "Travis will be here before we leave so no one will be missing any flights."

Things were still a little tense between Rena and James but he didn't want Scarlett or Minta to pick up on it so when she asked to hold Chandler he felt a sinking feeling in his stomach yet he forced some enthusiasm from deep within because it was the right thing to do in order to save face with his wife and mother-in-law.

The family continued to enjoy their last moments on the island over breakfast. Those last few moments would be overshadowed by a breaking news story. George looked up at the screen and tapped Minta on her arm to look up as well.

When George asked for the volume to be turned up because he could barely read the closed caption, Scarlett began to take notice.

Up above on the screen, the newscaster said, "We're sad to report that we've received word that Regina Montgomery, the First Lady of Wondrous Works Tabernacle Fellowship in Vino, California has died in a car accident. That car accident also claimed the life of their driver, Norris McDonald who had apparently been texting at the time of the accident. The Montgomery family has visited Chee Chee Island many times and spoken here so we want to express our sincerest condolences to Bishop Montgomery and his family during this tragic time. Several attempts have been made to reach the family but there hasn't been word of an official statement yet. As we get more information, we'll keep you updated here."

Jumping up from the table, Scarlett began screaming her disbelief, "What? No way, this isn't happening. She's dead? I just saw her weeks ago and now she's dead?"

Watching Scarlett completely melt down, as Minta ran over to comfort her, Derrick said under his breath, "Dead men tell no tales."

James held up his hand and said, "Not now dad."

George agreed, he said quietly, "But he's right James. She apparently didn't say anything and now she'll never be able to betray Scarlett and tell them about the baby, she kept her word and now she's taking it to her grave."

George and Derrick discussed the situation as James stood up to see about his wife. He pulled her from Minta's arms and held onto her and she sobbed uncontrollably. His heart bled for her as she mourned the loss of her former mother-in-law. Despite her issues with Carson, she and Regina had a special relationship, they shared a special bond. Scarlett was Regina's girl from the very start.

Feeling like she was at her breaking point, Scarlett felt like she couldn't take anymore. Too much too soon was happening and she was finding it hard to cope with each incident.

In her husband's arms she cried out, "Please make it stop, this is too much. Too much is going on and I feel like it's going on without me."

The other restaurant patrons looked on as Scarlett expressed her grief, they watched as if they were watching a scene from a movie.

As best as he could, James tried to comfort and assure her, "It's tough right now but you are tougher. You are the strongest woman I know but it's okay if you don't want to feel strong right now. I'm here to help you. Let me help you."

In a swift change of emotions, Scarlett quickly wiped her eyes pushed her hair back saying, "I now know what I need to do. Regina honored my request by not telling Carson about Chandler but now that she's gone, I need to honor her and do the right thing. Oh my God, she knew, she knew and yet she didn't say anything. She kept her word and now she's gone. She never even got a chance to see her grandson. I need to go back there….no, I have to go back there. I want to go to her funeral and pay my last respects and once I'm there, I'll tell Carson about Chandler and offer him the stem cells for his treatments."

Everyone at the table chimed in begging Scarlett to reconsider.

Minta grabbed up Scarlett and looked her eyeball to eyeball trying to connect with her daughter who had apparently lost it and said, "You don't owe them anything. If you want to offer him stem cells, that's fine but you don't have to go there to do that. I think that's a terrible idea. An open air apology doesn't absolve Carson from what he's done or the type of person he is. A snake with leukemia is still a snake and don't you forget that."

James shook his head and asked to speak with Scarlett privately, "Sweetheart, listen. This isn't a decision you can just make on your own….in case you have forgotten while grieving over another man's mother, I'm your husband. I'm really trying here Scarlett but you have got to meet me half way. And for the record, your husband doesn't like that idea at all. We never should have gone the first time and now you want to go back? Give me one good reason why I should subject our family to that turmoil?"

Scarlett tried to get James to calm down and she said, "James, you are simply amazing, I don't know what my life would be like without you in it. I love you and only you now I know you aren't threatened by Carson are you? You know I've been trying to figure out what to do and I see Regina's death as a sign. Carson needs help and if he doesn't get it, he might die and I don't want that to happen to that family if I can do something about it. You know, she appealed to me, woman to woman, mother to mother to help save her son's life and for all that she did for me, I feel like I owe her that. James, if I don't help him, my whole entire witness will be made a lie. Everything I've stood for and preached about with the walking and talking stuff will be considered straight up hypocrisy. Not to mention, I'm not sure that family could survive two deaths so close together like that."

James asked sharply, "But what about our family? I'm standing here questioning whether or not we'll be able to survive the Montgomerys?"

Scarlett took a deep breath and said, "I have a plan and yes, of course we will, we're going to be fine. You ask me all the time to trust you and now I'm asking you to have a little trust in me. We're going to be fine."

Both the Watsons and the Hartgroves had been discussing the matter themselves as James and Scarlett talked, they were ready for whatever might have been said.

Travis' van pulled up as Scarlett and James walked back over to their parents hand in hand, where James announced, "It's been settled, we're going to the funeral."

The unified parental quartet responded in kind and said, "And in that case, so are we."

Scarlett's eyes bulged out at their response, she questioned her parents, "We don't know when the funeral arrangements are going to be but what about Cole's graduation?"

George placed his hand on Scarlett's shoulder saying, "I'll talk with Cole; I know he'll understand. Not like his graduation isn't important but this is very important. You going out there impacts all of us."

Turning to her new in-laws, Scarlett said, "Not that I have a problem with it but why are you two going again?"

Rena looked at Scarlett and then James and said, "We're family and family sticks together. This situation can potentially impact our son and grandson and we want to be able to offer whatever support we can. Our calendar was clear anyway and your parents have insisted we stay with them until we leave for California so we'll be around to help out."

Scarlett hugged Rena as George and Derrick helped Travis out of the hospital van. Their boat to the airport would be arriving momentarily.

With the news of Regina's passing lingering on, Travis didn't get the welcome he was hoping for or the connection of family he longed for. Comparing his value to Scarlett's he thought, *"Even with a broken leg, the spotlight still seems to shine on her."*

CHAPTER 18

"Alright son, I knew you'd understand. We'll see you guys in a few days."

Walking over to the others, George pulled Minta aside while they waited for the luggage and said, "See there honey, Cole is fine. He said it's not like he hasn't walked the stage before. He's also fine with coming and staying at the house to look after Travis for us until we get back. He said if I didn't need him to do that, he'd be coming with us to California."

Minta smirked and said, "That's my boy."

George stood back with his chest poked out and said, "Yeah, he's one fine young man. I'm really proud of him, you know. Now, I need to get Travis on track and figure out what he wants to do with his life. Nevertheless, at such a young age, Cole has already gone farther than me. During my career I was able to manage several banks, while he already owns one. Isn't that something? I hate I'll miss his graduation but we'll party big when we get back, it'll be good to see him and Marissa."

Raising her eyebrow, Minta asked, "Marissa's coming?"

George looked at her squarely and said, "Yes Minta. You have a problem with that?"

Clearing her throat she said, "I don't know how I feel about them staying in our house without us being there."

Waving her off, George said, "Oh Minta please." He walked off to check on Travis.

With Travis' injury, George insisted that he come and recuperate at their house until his leg healed. With the extended invitation to the Hartgroves, Minta had to appear fine with Travis staying. How would it look to be hospitable to people she barely knew and not offer the same to her infirmed stepson. Prior to leaving for Chee Chee Island, George and Minta were enjoying the benefits of an empty nest, now they would be returning to a full house.

Derrick and Rena struggled to find their luggage, the carousel was on its way to making another round and they stood there with their necks extended checking and rechecking luggage tags.

Rena's theatrical groan made everyone turn and to look at her. She stared back saying, "What are y'all looking at? This better not be a case of lost luggage, I mean, what a way to get introduced to Jordan, huh?"

Derrick continued to search while Rena went on with her rants.

Still not feeling well, Scarlett strolled Chandler over to a bench while the others waited for the luggage. The flight seemed to have taken its toll on her, she felt weak and needed to sit down. Entertaining himself with the mobile on his carrier, Scarlett stared down at Chandler and smiled. She looked at him and thought, "*He's so perfect. In his world right now, he knows no wrong, no evil. He has no idea of the craziness going on in the world around him. Regina would have loved him.*"

"Penny for your thoughts pretty lady, ten bucks if they are dirty," James said.

Snapping out of her head back into reality, Scarlett stood and kissed James deeply, answering him saying, "Does that give you an idea of what I was thinking?"

Reaching into his pocket, James pulled out a twenty dollar bill and handed it Scarlett.

Laughing she said, "I thought you said ten dollars silly."

Licking his lips, James said, "Well uh young lady that kiss led me to believe your thoughts were real dirty so I thought I'd add in a little extra."

Playfully swatting at her husband, Scarlett narrowed her eyes onto James and said, "There's more where that came from. Can't you see the wheels turning in my head?"

James looked around and said, "My parents can find their own transportation, I'm not waiting on them any longer, my wife is thinking over here and I don't want her pretty little head to explode so I need to hurry up and get her home so I can examine some of these thoughts she's been having."

The couple pressed in close to each other and kissed again.

James looked around again and said, "That's it, time to go." He gathered up their luggage and hailed the next taxi.

CHAPTER 19

In comparison to the last two years, to the last forty-eight hours, Cayden-James felt like time had decided to stand still on his behalf. For the last two years, he'd found a way to manage but the two days leading up to his appeal, there were times he thought he saw the cell walls closing in on him. Thoughts of being incarcerated and having to come to terms with the fact he'd never see his mother again tore him into shreds. When people saw him they may have thought they were looking at Cayden-James Montgomery but to him, he'd been slashed into millions of tiny little pieces. He'd been willing to serve his time and repay his debt to society and not one time before had he gotten his hopes up about the appeal but now with Regina gone, he had to get out. He knew he couldn't stay another day.

Due to the circumstances, the warden allowed Christian and Bishop Montgomery into see Cayden-James before the appeal hearing.

Carson was unable to attend, Rebekkah was scheduled to be released from the hospital that day. Courtney decided to stay back and field phone calls and visitors along with keep watch over Mother Montgomery. In addition, her parents were set to arrive in town as well.

All three men, dressed in three-piece suits stood and looked at each other. It had been a while since they had all been face to face and now considering the grief they all shared, the warm and welcoming reunion they'd hoped for was exchanged with tears and long faces.

Cayden-James held onto his father and brother as he cried saying, "I can't believe she's gone, I can't believe she's really gone."

The knock at the door alerted them time was nigh, the hearing was about to begin.

Bishop offered up a prayer for a favorable outcome of the hearing, saying, "Lord, the heart of the king is in your hand; You can turn whichever way you please[4]. Lord, I ask you to turn his heart in my son's favor. His time is up here Lord, we need him home. We need him at Wondrous Works. In Jesus' name. Amen."

Since Regina's death, every time Christian heard the name Wondrous Works he had a negative response to it. Bishop ignored him and kept on going.

Inside the courtroom, Cayden-James' defense team presented their case for appeal as did the prosecution.

Upon hearing both sides, the judge asked if there was any victim testimony and interestingly enough, while there had been one name scheduled to speak the week before, the victim declined their opportunity to speak.

The judge called for a recess to go over the information. Within a half hour, he was back to render his decision.

Asking Cayden-James to stand he said with crossed hands and through a stoical voice, he said, "Mr. Montgomery, you have a brilliant mind that got you caught up in the snares of greed. I know you to come from a religious family so I'll try and give you a bit of advice. I think this comes from one of the Proverbs but greedy people, those who get unjust gain bring trouble to their families, to their houses, to their communities. But the person who can't be paid to do wrong will live. From what I've read in your

---

4 **Proverbs 21:1**: "The king's heart is in the hand of the Lord, as are the watercourses; He turns it whichever way He wills." (**AMP**)

file and have heard from those who have watched you over the last two years, you have been of exemplary behavior and have paid restitution and made apology to all of your victims. You finished your course of study and received your degree. Therefore, in light of all of the evidence and the timing of this hearing, I bid you to go and do as the scripture has said and that is to live young man. As you go forward in life, I'd admonish you to use your powers for good and not for evil. Cayden-James Elijah Montgomery you are now free to go."

Christian hopped over the bench and grabbed up his brother, they'd won the appeal. The moment was bittersweet for Bishop because he thought back on the conversations he and Regina had about bringing her baby home. She'd talked to her husband about bringing him home like she had done when he was a baby. He was now headed home but she wasn't there to see him.

CHAPTER 20

The Montgomery estate was filled with people from all over. The phone rang so much, Courtney decided to turn off the ringer, she felt like if it was important, they'd get calls on their cell phones.

Feeling her phone buzz, she looked down at the screen to see a message from Christian, **"He's free, we're coming home baby**." Making the announcement, everyone in the house cheered with sounds of applause, a few thank you Jesus, and a round of praise the Lords.

Since the day Regina had passed, Mother Montgomery had been staying at the house. Courtney was headed to tell her the news when the doorbell rang. Opening the door, a young woman jumped inside the front door with her arms in the air, exclaiming, "I'm here." Hugging on Courtney, she said, "You must be Courtney, sorry I missed the wedding but I saw the pictures, you were a beautiful bride. Now where are my cousins and my Uncle Bishop? I flew here as fast as I could to be here with them."

Courtney's increased difficulty in finding the right words left her standing in the door way with her mouth wide opened. Shutting the door around the bags of luggage, Courtney did manage to finally say, "Am I supposed to know who you are?"

Stopping in her tracks, the young lady turned and said, "Everyone should know who I am…especially you. I know my cousins and my aunt talk about me all of the time. In case you didn't know, I'm Cherie Monet Van Pelt but I go by Cherie Monet."

Courtney put two and two together saying, "Hey there, yes, it's so nice to finally meet you, I'm sorry it's been a rough few days and I didn't recognize you without all of the makeup and the hair."

Cherie Monet Van Pelt, also known as Cherie Monet was Regina's niece, a gospel singer who had just finished up an International tour. Cherie was raised in and out of the Montgomery house after Regina's sister, Carolyn died from breast cancer. Regina took Cherie in and looked after her like one of her own children, she and Cayden-James were only a few months apart.

Courtney said, "I was about to go check on Grandma Montgomery, do you want to go say hi? I was also going to let her know about Cayden-James."

Raising her hands up in the air, in the raise the roof motion, Cherie said, "Yes, I got the text from Christian. They should be here in a couple of hours and I can't wait to see those guys." Walking down the hallway, Cherie continued, "I'm glad to be home but I hate why I'm here."

Entering the room, Mother Montgomery was seated in the chair by the bed watching television. Upon laying eyes on Cherie she said, "Hmmm, look at what the cat drug in."

Plopping down on the bed, Cherie exclaimed, "Grandma Montgomery; I'm touched." Leaning over to kiss her on the cheek, Cherie said, "Nice to see you too Grandma."

Seated in her chair, Mother Montgomery crossed her arms at the elbows and cocked her head to the side as she took inspection of Cherie and said, "I don't like what I'm seeing on you girl."

Cherie felt the hairs on the back of her neck stand up at the sound of Mother Montgomery's discernment.

Courtney broke up the moment and said, "Oh Grandma Montgomery, I came in here to tell you that Cayden-James won his appeal and they are all headed home. They should be here in a couple of hours."

Raising two frail hands slightly, Mother Montgomery said softly, "Thank you Lord for sending Regina's baby home." A lone tear fell from her face, she unfolded a lace handkerchief and dabbed her face and said, "I've been sitting here praying all morning; I knew he'd win."

Cherie stood up and said, "I'm hungry, I'm going to go see if I can find something to eat."

Courtney said, "I'll go with you." Looking over at Mother Montgomery, Courtney said, "Call me if you need anything."

Mother Montgomery nodded her head and the young ladies left.

Inside the kitchen, Courtney and Cherie turned around to see Carson and Rebekkah walking in through the back door.

Cherie squealed and ran up to Carson and hugged and kissed over him saying, "I'm so glad to see you brothercousin, you sharp shooter you." Glancing over at Rebekkah she said, "And you must be Rebekkah, the one with two k's."

Christian had already filled in Cherie about the shooting and everything else going on. He was typically her line of communication.

Cherie knew that Carson's clenched jaw indicated he was annoyed with her as he often times was, but she knew that Carson was oftentimes annoyed with everyone outside of himself.

Standing next to Carson, Rebekkah stood with her arm in a cast and sling and he said, "Rebekkah, this is my cousin, Cherie, she's been away singing…I guess you could say she's like a pesky little sister type. We actually try not to let too many people know she's connected with us."

Rebekkah smiled and said to Cherie, "It's really nice to meet you, I've heard a lot about you. Oh and by the way, I really enjoyed your last album."

Looking around the kitchen, Rebekkah was trying to process how she felt being back in the Montgomery home. The last time she was there, her visit with Regina was less than warm. Regina compared Rebekkah to the woman mentioned in Proverbs 7:27[5]. To now be standing in her home without her being there was different. While Regina's belongings were still there, her spirit was definitely missing from the home.

Noticing the distance between Rebekkah and Courtney, Cherie sat down on one of the bar stools and said, "I thought you two knew each other."

Speaking with light sarcasm, Courtney looked directly at Rebekkah and said, "We do or at least I thought we did. But tell me, how am I supposed to strike up a conversation with someone who just up and walked out on their family and then pretend like just because they got shot, everything is supposed to be back to normal. How does that work?"

Standing in the expansive kitchen, Courtney decided it was no longer big enough for the four of them so she walked out.

Cherie spun around on the barstool and said, "Well, I guess that went well."

Unmoved by Courtney's dramatic exit, Carson sat down at the table and asked, "So Cherie, how long are you planning on staying this time?"

---

[5] **Proverbs 7:27**: "Her house is the way to hell, going down to the chambers of death." (**KJV**)

Pulling her baseball cap down lower over her face, Cherie answered, "I'm not sure. I guess I'll play it by ear; I'm actually waiting on a call from my agent."

Since being at the hospital with Rebekkah, Carson seemed to have found some renewed strength from somewhere, he stood and helped Rebekkah up, tapping Cherie on her hat saying, "Well kid, it's good to have you home. Mother was looking forward to seeing you so even though she's not here, I know she's up there smiling knowing that you're back."

Carson and Rebekkah walked out of the kitchen, leaving Cherie to herself. Hearing that her aunt was excited to see her come home brought tears to her eyes. She wondered, "*I wonder if she would have felt the same way about me had she known what's going on with me.*"

Lowering her head on the table, Cherie began to cry.

CHAPTER 21

"So, how are you doing?"

"I'm surviving and how about you?"

"I'm fine Delores…well actually I'm not and that's why I'm calling you."

Delores switched her phone to the other ear, "Here we go again, what is it Dottie?"

Dottie and Delores were sisters, they were two parts of a third cord that shouldn't have been broken, they were born triplets but their other sister, Daphne died when they were children from a poisonous snake bite.

Delores was the feistier one where Dottie was more delicate, so when Delores said, "Stop beating around the bush, what do you need?" Dottie jumped.

Answering slowly, Dottie said, "I was just wondering if…"

Creating impatience in Delores, she breathed a heavy sigh and said, "You were wondering if what Dottie?"

Dottie was in the process of turning what was supposed to be a quick phone call into a long, drawn-out event and Delores was becoming highly irritated.

Dottie spoke up and said, "Alright, alright. Please don't curse me out but I was wondering if you thought you might would want to possibly come home for a small, teeny tiny visit?"

Delores sucked in the air and blew it right back out of her cheeks, "Now Dottie you already know the answer to that question. Why would I do that?"

Dottie sounded hopeful, "I just thought that since you're in that house all alone you might want to come and visit your sister."

"If my sister wants a visit, she can come here to see me," Delores shared.

Trying to reason, Dottie said, "That's not the only reason I thought you might would come."

"What else is there?" Delores asked.

Dottie took a deep breath, "An investor has been stopping by, calling me, and I feel like down-right harassing me about the inn and I've tried handling it on my own but I need your help."

In a stern tone, Delores responded, "I told you I don't want anything to do with that property. You can do whatever you want to with it Dottie."

"But it's half yours Delores," Dottie argued.

Delores sat quietly on the phone.

Delores and Dottie's parents were grape pickers in the old wine country but they didn't pick grapes their entire lives. They were conservative with what little they had and they saved what they could afford. Over many years and late in life, their father realized his dream and was able to buy a small vineyard that he turned into a boutique winery and bed and breakfast. The property was willed to both Delores and Dottie as equal owners. Delores tried to give her share away to Dottie making her the sole owner but she wouldn't accept it.

When Delores left Vino, she vowed to never return.

Dottie broke the silence, "The inn is becoming too much for me to handle on my own and I was thinking it would be nice for us to reconnect by running it and figuring out what to do about this investor. It's beautiful this time of year, you remember don't you sis?"

Delores still sat quietly.

Still trying to be convincing, Dottie tried one more approach by saying, "I miss you Delores. Let's face it, we're both single and our children are all grown. I think it's time you gave up the ghost of Vino's past. Trust me, things are different."

Sitting up in her chair, Delores finally spoke and asked, "What do you mean things are different."

"Oh, you haven't heard? I'm sure by now you've heard the news, right?" Dottie asked.

"What news Dottie?"

Placing a hand over her mouth, Dottie realized Delores didn't know.

With another glimmer of hope in her voice, Dottie softly shared the news of Regina's passing by saying, "Regina Montgomery is dead. She died a few days ago in a tragic car accident."

Delores gasped, "Oh no, that's horrible news. I'm so sorry to hear that but that changes nothing for me Dottie."

Dottie smirked and said, "Well it should. If my reasons won't get you here, maybe this will. From what I hear, the sharks are already circling him, they are coming out of the woodwork honey. They haven't even put that poor woman in the ground yet and the women are lining up trying to place their bid to become the next 'first lady' in his life. Now, he is still a good looking man so I don't think he'll be single for long. However, according to what the people say, he's not paying attention to any of it. I mean can you blame him, he just lost his wife for goodness sakes. But you should understand that, you know, losing Charles and all."

Delores interrupted her sister, "Stop it. I don't want to hear any more about this. I'm done having this conversation with you. I can't listen to any more of this. Thanks for calling but listen to me, I seriously don't care what you do with the inn or what you decide to do about the investor. You love it more than I do so I know you'll make the right decision."

CHAPTER 22

The prelude music in the sanctuary was playing at an upbeat tempo. Bishop Montgomery expressed, Regina was a lively person and she'd often times told him if she ever proceeded him in death, that she didn't want a sad and dreary service. She would tell him, I've spent my whole life in church, believing that when I die, it should be a time of rejoicing so if I die before you, make sure we have real good church and a high time of rejoicing.

Thousands upon thousands were gathered to pay their last respects to Regina, a woman who loved the Lord and was a true example of lifestyle evangelism until the very end.

As her pictures scrolled across the screens, the people's chatter was filled with beautiful memories of a life well lived.

The Hartgrove/Watson entourage arrived and Scarlett made the same arrangements with Brother Oscar Robinson she'd made previously. She didn't want to detract from the funeral. She felt like she'd address the family later.

Regina Montgomery had brought people out from the North, South, East, and West. Every type of denomination and religion was represented. From local officials to state and national dignitaries, they were there on her behalf.

Just like a regular Sunday worship service, Regina's funeral was being streamed live. Many were tuned in but two in particular watched from their respective homes, Ali Joyner and Delores Bolton Mosley.

Inside the sanctuary, those in attendance stood and sang songs of high praise, such as "When the Saints Go Marching In" as Regina's family entered in, dressed in all white, two by two.

Several family members received a few stares and gawks from the crowd such as, Carson and Rebekkah being together, a freed Cayden-James, and the prodigal niece, Cherie.

Due to the magnitude of the service, Bishop Montgomery didn't want to allow for expressions because he knew the service would never end. Some family and friends had a chance to speak the night before at the wake but in order to honor Regina's wishes instead of a traditional repass, Bishop had planned for a huge celebration of life event at the estate after the service and more words were to be shared there. The order of the program would follow as outlined with a few of Regina's favorite songs, some of her favorite scriptures, liturgical dancing, and eulogistical remarks. Courtney's father, Bishop Davis, insisted on giving those remarks and Bishop bestowed upon him the honor.

The service was flowing nicely and Rena was up in the room in awe. For her first time to have ever been in church, her first experience would be at Wondrous Works memorializing the one and only Regina Montgomery.

Bishop Davis stood up and addressed the bereaved family, the congregation, and he looked up above and even addressed Regina, saying, "Congratulations sister, you made it home."

He acknowledged the fact that others may have been more qualified to speak but he made it clear that it didn't matter how long he'd known the family, the quantity of years didn't matter, what mattered was the quality and the pureness of the fellowship. He expressed at how being co-laborers in the ministry, the two families had been a constant source of support.

Preparing to begin his message, he said, "I've preached more funerals than I can count and at most of them, there are things said that I'm sure most of you have heard. Such as, to be absent from the body is to be present with the Lord. Now, I've said that many times before but when I got the news about my dear sister and the circumstances surrounding the accident, in my natural mind, I questioned why her. But I have to tell you that God dealt with me and for the first time ever, those words came alive more to me. Here me when I say this, for those of you hurting right now, our dear sister didn't suffer. For, as soon as she closed her eyes, she woke up in the arms of Jesus. I bet if you could ask her if she wanted to come back she'd tell you no. This isn't a time to be sad but a time of celebration."

Applause was heard from around the sanctuary.

Rena clapped and said, "I have no idea what he's talking about or if I even believe half of what he's saying but this is riveting."

Scarlett giggled a little at Rena while everyone else kept looking ahead.

Bishop Davis continued on, "I'm here to offer words of encouragement and if we can quickly turn to Matthew 8:23-27 and indulge me for a few moments, I promise I'll be out of your way[6]. Here in the text, on that particular day, Jesus' day was filled with ministry, He'd healed leprosy, brought healthy restoration to a young boy and Peter's mother-in-law, and drove out demonic spirits from many who were sick. As a result, throngs of people started gathering around him and He gave his disciples orders to cross to the other side which was the Sea of Galilee. By the time He came on the scene, the Sea of Galilee was the crowned jewel of the fishing industry and several of His disciples were Galilean

---

[6] **Mathew 8:23-27**: "23 And after He got into the boat, His disciples followed Him. 24 And suddenly, behold, there arose a violent storm on the sea, so that the boat was being covered up by the waves; but He was sleeping. 25 And they went and awakened Him, saying, Lord, rescue and preserve us! We are perishing! 26 And He said to them, Why are you timid and afraid, O you of little faith? Then He got up and rebuked the winds and the sea, and there was a great and wonderful calm (a perfect peaceableness).
27 And the men were stunned with bewildered wonder and marveled, saying, What kind of Man is this, that even the winds and the sea obey Him!" (**AMP**)

fishermen. Before crossing over, two of the disciples shared with Jesus that they were ready to follow him, Jesus, however, gave them a little something to think about, quite direct, He was letting them know there's a cost to following him and sometimes difficult costs and great sacrifice. Sister Regina, followed Christ, she was fully aware of the costs, she knew there would be no earthly rewards, she knew that some of her decisions might be unpopular, she knew that some of her other loyalties might compete for attention, and that her leisure time might be reduced, but yet and still, she followed Him. Now with all that went on that day, He needed a little break from all of the excitement so when He got on the boat, anyone choosing to follow Him needed to leave all the excuses behind and jump on board."

Everyone was plugged into Bishop Davis' words, he was starting to find his stride.

Walking across the stage he said, "I want to share a little context here, when you hear the Sea of Galilee, I'm sure that makes you think of a gigantic body of water. However, in comparison it was more like a lake as it is approximately 13 miles long and 6 miles wide. It lies almost 700 feet below the Mediterranean Sea, and its greatest depth is 200 feet. It is said to resemble the shape of a harp. Now, I hope that sets a picture in your mind because here is something interesting. The Sea of Galilee is an unusual body of water in the sense that sudden and violent storms with up to twenty foot waves can appear without little to no warning. Based on the climate there, oftentimes, the collision of warm and cold air, occur frequently which causes the storms. So, in case you were wondering, it wasn't that they got in the boat ignoring the signs of a storm brewing over the ocean but they were caught out there without any warning and the potential for danger was great."

Back at the podium, with detailed precision Bishop Davis had laid the foundation for his message and was now about to deliver, he carried on by saying, "According to the text, it says and suddenly a violent storm arose and the boat was covered up by the waves; I mentioned earlier that these waves could get up to twenty feet. Now could you imagine being out on a boat in the middle of a storm and the person you are supposed to be following is asleep? Well, that's what happened. Jesus was knocked out in the middle of a storm, in the middle of a storm, He took a nap. Let me know you're still here with me and say, He took a nap. Picture the scene, Jesus napping, disciples panicking…in the middle of a storm and a violent one at that. These were people who were in the boat with Jesus and yet, they weren't exempt from the storm. Just because we choose to follow Him doesn't preclude us from the sudden storms in life. People have grabbed a hold of this idea that those who follow Christ will now be problem free and that just simply isn't the case. For the reason in which we are here today, we can clearly see that this sudden storm we are experiencing with the loss of Regina that things happen. However, here's what I want to point out, while the disciples had witnessed many miracles performed by Jesus, most of them right there at the Sea of Galilee they panicked in this storm. This unexpected turn of events, frightened them terribly. As experienced sailors and fishermen they knew it was dangerous to be out there; what they did not know was that Christ could control the forces of nature. They didn't know He could speak a word to the storm and make it behave. Just like the disciples in our text, we often encounter storms in our life, where we feel God can't or won't work, or better yet, is asleep. However, when we truly understand who God is, we will realize that He not only controls both the storms of nature but also the storms of our troubled hearts. Jesus' power that calmed that storm can also help us deal with the problems we face and He's willing to help if we only ask. Then we'll be like those disciples standing in awe of him saying, what kind of man is?"

Around the sanctuary, many were moved by Bishop Davis' words, he closed his notes and began to close by saying, "My fellow brothers and sisters, there are times in our lives where things happen that are simply beyond our control and in these moments, we shouldn't be like the disciples and replace our faith with fear but we should turn to Him in the light of His power and sovereignty. Most times, storms come to point us back to him. It may feel like it but we haven't lost Regina; I know exactly where she is. She's doing better now than she's ever done in her life. Now, I'm not even going to pretend and make like this doesn't hurt, so I know some tears will be shed and there will be some rough days ahead but if I can offer any words of encouragement to you today, I'd say storms don't last always and even though Jesus was asleep during the storm, he heard the cries from his disciples. I submit to you all today that according to Isaiah 59:1, "Surely the arm of the Lord is not too short to save, nor His ear too dull to hear. Always remember, for we don't sorrow as those who have no hope because we know that to be absent from the body is to be present with the Lord. Church, you and I have our hope in glory and glory forever more. Family and friends…let's be encouraged."

Tapping a loose fist against his heart, Bishop Montgomery looked up at Bishop Davis with soft eyes and mouthed, "Thank you."

CHAPTER 23

The Montgomery family hugged and greeted those who came to participate in the grave side service before returning to the home for the celebration.

The line to speak with Bishop Montgomery snaked through the cemetery. He decided he would only speak to a few more people and then he'd be ready to leave.

Standing under a wide brimmed white hat with designer sunglasses and a blinged out sling, Rebekkah felt a tug on her arm as she stood and people watched off in the distance. The tug and the whispered voice was familiar, she heard, "I knew it…how did I know you'd be here with him; I can't believe you."

Turning around slowly, not wanting to cause a scene, Rebekkah said in a restrained tone, "Oh, you can't believe me, I still can't believe you left me. Godfrey, you do remember that you were the one that left, correct?"

Trying to maintain his composure, Godfrey answered coolly, "Yes Rebekkah and you know why I left."

"Oh yeah, now I remember…you got all convicted and self-righteous. This was our plan and you bailed out on me but I learned a long time ago that one monkey don't stop the show and especially a show where I have a leading role."

Pleading his case, Godfrey said, "Rebekkah, this isn't right and I was trying to get you to understand that. In the beginning it seemed like a good enough plan but over time I started realizing what we were trying to do was wrong. Hey, I'm sorry; I can't help it that I started feeling guilty."

Blending in with the crowd, Rebekkah snapped at Godfrey, "You feel guilty, I don't. Nothing has changed, I'm still going through with the plan, in fact, with what I'm carrying, the stakes just got even higher."

Godfrey pulled at his ear and asked, "I have no idea what that's supposed to mean but hey, there's something different about you. What happened to your arm?"

Positioning her body at an angle instead of facing him head on, Rebekkah scoffed and said, "It means whatever I want it to mean. Oh this, it's not a big deal, just think of it as a battle wound. But I want you to answer me this, if you were so done with the Montgomerys, where have you been and why are you here today?"

Godfrey checked his watch, "Look, I can't get into it here but long story short, when I left you, I was in bad shape spiritually. I knew I couldn't go back to Wondrous Works and look them in their eyes knowing what I knew so I went somewhere else. When my dad was younger, growing up at Wondrous Works, he was friends with the Montgomery boys, Bishop and his brother, Claude. Knowing I wasn't going back to Wondrous Works, I called my dad and he suggested I reach out to Claude Montgomery for counseling. I must've showed up at the right time because his chief of security had just resigned and since he knew my dad and told him about my work at Wondrous Works, he gave me the job. Interestingly enough, he hasn't seen his brother in years but he wanted to be here for Regina's funeral today so I'm here accompanying him. Now, I'm not a fan of her son but she was a fine woman."

Using her one good hand, Rebekkah stepped up, pointing her finger in Godfrey's face, saying, "You haven't told him anything have you? I hope you haven't been trying to cleanse your soul and getting things right with God by spilling the beans about our plan...have you?"

Placing one finger on his lip, Godfrey thought for a second before he said, "No, I haven't but you know what, you could stand to do a little spiritual cleansing yourself. Do I hate Carson, yes, I do. Did I want to take him down a notch or two or three, yes, I did. But listen to me, stop this now while you still can, I'm telling you this is a bad idea."

For a brief moment, Rebekkah dropped the tough girl act and asked the question she really wanted to know, she lowered her head and said, "But I thought you loved me and that we were in this together…don't you love me?"

Resisting the urge to grab Rebekkah and hug her, Godfrey spoke in short-tempered tones, "Yes, I do love you. I wish I could hold you right now, you know it's killing me to see you with him, right? I've been going crazy not being with you but I just couldn't keep it up, you have to understand that; I need you to understand that. Listen, we can still be together but not like this Rebekkah."

Quickly returning to her previous disposition, she said, "I won't do it, I'm not abandoning the plan. Now that I'm back, it's only going to be a matter of time before he tries to get me to sign that prenuptial agreement. I've come too far and with or without you, I'm going to get my hands on some of that Montgomery money and when I do, don't come calling me either. Goodness gracious Godfrey, we were this close and you ruined it now I have some more leg work to do."

For the years that Godfrey served Carson, his loyalty turned into treachery, Godfrey despised Carson. He and his duplicitous partner, Rebekkah devised a plan to infiltrate the Montgomery family

Noticing the family starting to disperse, Rebekkah looked at Godfrey and said, "Good-bye Godfrey, I need to go and be with my husband, he looks like he needs me."

Rebekkah walked off as Godfrey stood feeling helpless with his hands in his pocket. Feeling Godfrey's eyes on her body, she slinked it in next to Carson's and they walked towards the cars for the family.

CHAPTER 24

"So are you really ready to do this sweetheart?"

Scarlett squeezed James' hand as they traveled down the road leading up to the Montgomery compound. Passing the makeshift memorial at the crash site, Scarlett's eyes widened as she took notice of the huge display of flowers, gifts, and balloons, all left on the side of the road for Regina and Norris.

George followed all of the other cars lining up to get onto the grounds. They'd made a quick stop after the funeral to do a babysitter switch. Minta had decided to stay at the hotel with Chandler during the funeral while Rena would stay during the at home celebration. Minta wanted to be with Scarlett when she approached Carson for the first time.

Stepping out of the car, the Hartgrove/Watson entourage was ready for whatever might come their way, they were united in the support for Scarlett.

There were some who recognized Scarlett but not certain enough to stop her to say hello, they just speculated as she and her family walked up to the back yard where the party was taking place. The elegant white canopy topped tent indicated a grand affair was in high gear and Scarlett was doing her best not to let her jitters get the best of her. There were a lot of emotions and thoughts running through her as she was on the grounds of her former in-laws where she'd spent a considerable amount of time. Her thoughts would not keep her hostage for long. Standing at the edge of the steps to enter the event, Scarlett turned around as she felt a tap on her shoulder and heard, 'Excuse me, Ms. Scarlett?"

At the sound of Scarlett's name, everyone turned around, George, Minta, James, Derrick, and also Scarlett, who answered by saying, "Yes."

John Dixon, Carson's armor bearer said, "Would you mind following me? There's someone who'd like to speak with you."

Glances were traded amongst the group, uncertain of what was about to happen, Scarlett held onto James' hand and said, "Okay, lead the way."

Inside the home, Scarlett walked through trying to stay focused by not looking around because the one time she did, she caught sight of a picture she was in with Regina and the twinge she felt in her chest was competing with the pangs she was already feeling from knowing at some point she was about to come face to face with her ex-husband, Carson.

John led them to the study where Carson and Rebekkah where awaiting them. For Scarlett, that point was now, walking into the study, Carson stood up and faced her.

It had been months since he'd last seen her and so much had happened in between that time. Looking at her walk in, with a nervous stomach, his chin quivered. In order for him to do what he did to her, he had to come to a place where he'd disconnected from her in order to justify his actions. For months, he wondered what he'd do if he saw her, what he might say, or how he might respond. Upon seeing her, for the first time since she'd been gone, his brain connected to his heart, what he'd done. To him, she was more beautiful than he remembered and without him, she looked happy.

As the Hartgrove/Watson clan filed into the room, it seemed as if the air in the room stopped moving for a minute. Scarlett and James stood together with George, Minta, and Derrick standing behind them.

Carson took the bold step to break the silence and said, "And here I thought this might be awkward. How are you Scarlett?"

Replaying the events from the night he kicked her out, to the day she saw Regina, to the Sunday he confessed, Scarlett felt as if time was slowing down. Seeking reassurance from James she looked at him and he squeezed her hand, looking Carson squarely in his face she said, "I couldn't be better."

With all of their eyes on him, his cheeks burned. He wasn't sure if it was because of his dishonorable conduct or his improper and despicable acts towards Scarlett or if it was from the fire that blazed from Minta's eyes. Notwithstanding the reason, he offered for them to all have a seat.

Sitting down with strong posture, Scarlett asked, "How did you know I was here?"

Carson hitched his breath and said, "A member of the staff noticed you when you all drove in and then called me."

Taking several quick glimpses, Scarlett performed a full body scan of Rebekkah. She sat wondering if by now seeing her did she still hold bitterness and hatred in her heart for the woman who had stolen her husband.

Setting the record straight, Scarlett spoke up and said, "Well Carson, this is my husband, Dr. James Hartgrove and we are so sorry about your family's loss. You know my parents and this is my father-in-law, Dr. Derrick Hartgrove. We wanted to come by and share our condolences."

Digesting her words, he spoke without hesitation, Carson said, "She was your family too but I thank you." Standing, Carson extended his hand to James, his father, and George and Minta and greeted them kindly.

Turning towards Rebekkah, he said, "Well, since we're doing introductions, this is my wife, Rebekkah."

Scarlett sat with a blank stare and slacked expression as she thought, "*I thought she left him. Oh well, that's none of my business. I guess you never really know what goes on in people's marriages?*"

In the few days Rebekkah had been back, Carson had started to take a little more interest in his condition. He'd increased his water intake and changed up some of his dietary needs such as eating more fruits and vegetables so he was looking a little better than the last time Scarlett saw him at the church.

Unaware Scarlett had witnessed his confession, he tried to turn on his charm, he said, "Scarlett, mother would've been so happy to have seen you. Considering, this was very nice of you to come here." With a smirk, he asked, "But tell me, was I that bad you felt like you needed to bring a posse with you?"

Trying to stay out of the exchange, Minta fought the urge to blurt out how bad he really was.

Scarlett didn't need Minta to say it, she did, smiling, she said, "Yes, you were that bad." Looking at Rebekkah, she said laughing, "Buyer beware."

Scarlett's joke mixed with truth provided the room with some much needed light-heartedness.

Rebekkah responded with a smile and light nod.

Everyone laughed before the mood turned serious again.

Sitting up on the edge of her seat, Scarlett decided to go ahead and do what she came there to do, she wasn't interested in spending any more time with Carson other than what was needed. She opened up by saying, "First of all, your mother meant more to me than you'll ever know…literally."

With a tilt of the head, Carson said, "What do you mean by that?"

Clearing her throat, Scarlett looked around at her support team, James gave her a slight nod. She started down the path of explanation, she said, "Well, I saw your mother recently. Through chance, she found out where I was. When I saw her she told me you had been diagnosed with Leukemia."

Rebekkah shifted in her seat while Carson leaned away from Scarlett and said, "Interesting."

Taking easy breaths, Scarlett said, "When she left, unbeknownst to any of you, James and I flew out here and attended a service at Wondrous Works."

Carson's head flinched back slightly, he asked, "Which Sunday?"

"Yeah, that…Sunday," Scarlett confirmed.

Carson shook his lowered head as he reflected back on his high noon confession, pounding his fists into his thighs, he whispered an emotional onslaught of heartfelt apologies, he constantly said, "I'm so sorry."

Unsure of what to do, Rebekkah turned and rubbed his shoulders in an effort to comfort a shameful Carson.

Giving him a moment to collect himself, Scarlett took in and absorbed the scene and became acutely aware of her powerful advantage.

Adjusting her position in her chair and moving even closer to James, Scarlett said, "So here's the thing, when you removed me from our marriage, I wasn't the only one you cut off. What I didn't know at the time was that I left here pregnant. I recently gave birth to a baby boy. Here's the tricky part though, biologically, that baby boy is yours. However, based on how you sent me off from here, giving me instructions on how to disappear and start a new life, I did just that. As a result, legally, the baby belongs to my husband, James. He was with me through my pregnancy, the birth, and up through today with his day to day care….he is his father."

Scarlett's words penetrated throughout Carson's entire body and everyone sat quietly, watching how those words were going to impact him.

Scarlett continued, "When I saw your mother, she mentioned to me that you could benefit from a stem cell transplant and call it luck or whatever you might think, I have an account with my local cord blood bank…I saved the baby's cord blood. Supposedly, it contains cells that can help with conditions such as yours. I came here to Vino to pay my last respects to Regina and to also tell you about this. I don't want or need anything from you and if you're interested you can have the cord blood for your treatments but otherwise that is it…that's all I'm offering."

Reaching his hand out towards Scarlett, Carson quickly pulled it back as if he wasn't worthy of her touch any longer. His shoulders curled over his chest as he quaked with repressed sobs. In a pleading tone, he verbalized responsibility for his actions and begged for everyone's forgiveness. The pangs of guilt and consciousness opened him up to the reality that the balance of power had shifted significantly in Scarlett's favor. He felt powerless of the present and the future. He knew he was in no position to ask anything of her yet he did ask through tears, "Can I ask what you decided to name him?"

Those there for Scarlett were on edge with her answering specifics about the baby but they all sat quietly as Scarlett handled herself flawlessly.

With a smile, she said, "I tend to call him perfect but his name is Chandler Eugene Watson Hartgrove."

Carson's lip trembled realizing the significance of his son's name. He swallowed the harsh reality of his actions, he understood that terms were now being dictated to him based on terms he enacted with her.

Taking a gamble he asked, "Is there a chance I could possibly see him?"

Both Minta and George cleared their throats in an effort to voice their displeasure without saying a word.

Scarlett looked at James for direction and as a gesture of good faith, James pulled out his phone and showed Carson a picture of Chandler saying, "Here he is man."

The flutter in his heart while looking at Chandler reminded him why he so desperately wanted a child in the first place. He longed for an opportunity to reproduce and see an extension of himself and now he was looking at his seed, even if it was in megapixels. Seeing Chandler also jolted his memory about his pending arrival with Rebekkah.

Purposely closing his eyes, as if to process everything, he decided to make the best of the situation, he looked at Rebekkah's stomach and then at Chandler's picture one last time and handed the phone back to James.

Hoisting himself up from the loveseat he shared with Rebekkah, Carson stood and walked over to George and Minta. Standing in front of them, he offered his hand, apologized, and solemnly asked for their forgiveness. Turning his attention to Derrick, he extended his hand and said, "Thanks for being here for them." Making his way to James he said, "I thank God for you. I'm glad she found you. Thank you for taking care of her and the baby."

Both Scarlett and Rebekkah's mouths were dropped open as they watched Carson humble himself in front of everyone, for the both of them, this was a first.

In front of Scarlett, he sat back down with Rebekkah and said, "Scarlett, there are no words to describe the kind of person you are. One that comes to mind is selfless. For all that I did to you, you could have easily written me off and never thought of me again. You could have gone on with your life and never told me about Chandler, yet you're here. I know I've probably caused you so much pain and heartache and still you have come in peace and wanting to help me out. I appreciate your offer for the stem cells, I really do, but I'm not going to accept them. I don't want to cause you any more trouble, you finally look happy and I don't want to interfere with that after all I've done to you, I owe you that. Now, am I saying I don't want to have anything to do with my son? No, I'm not. Do I feel like I'm giving him up? In a way I do but if I look at it, my actions caused this and I realize that based on what I did, I essentially gave him up. I have another chance at a cord blood transfusion because Rebekkah is pregnant and hopefully somewhere down the road, you and James will allow me to have some type of relationship with Chandler but you have my word, I'm not going to cause any more problems for you."

Pressing one hand to her stomach, Scarlett struggled to find the right words and speak, she showed a level of kinship with Carson by reaching for his hand and patting it saying, "Thank you."

James stood up and said, "Thank you and congratulations. At the appropriate time, his mother and I will be in touch with you."

CHAPTER 25

Popping his head into the doorway, Cole said, "Hey man, Marissa and I are going to order a pizza and watch a movie would you like to join us?"

Travis looked up from his book and answered his younger brother by saying, "Sure, sounds like fun. Which movie are you watching?"

"I'm not real sure, I'm just going to go see what's out there and pick up a couple. You like anything in particular?" Cole asked.

Answering quickly, Travis said, "I'll be fine with whatever you get man."

Cole smiled and said, "So you don't have a type a movie you like?"

"Yeah, I do. I mean, you know I like all guy type movies, I was just saying I'll watch whatever you get. I'm already the third wheel, I'm just trying not to be a nuisance. I know you had to miss your graduation in order to be here with me so I'm not trying to make it any harder on you guys."

Stepping completely into Travis' temporary accommodations, he said, "Yeah, yeah, I hear what you're saying but it's no big deal. My dad called and said he needed my help so here I am."

Travis checked his phone and asked, "Have you heard from George today?"

Sitting down on the bed, Cole said, "Yeah, I got a text the funeral was over and they were headed to the Montgomery estate. He said that funeral lasted four hours, can you believe that?"

"Four hours huh? I can't even imagine, the only funeral I've ever been to was my mother's and it only lasted an hour. Do you think Scarlett and James have anything to worry about letting that guy know about Chandler?"

Staring off into space, Cole said, "It's hard to say right now. I know what, I have a lot of respect for my sister because I can't say I'd be doing what she's doing if it were my kid. She feels she's doing the right thing so I can't be mad at that. By her doing the right thing by Carson, hopefully, he'll do the right thing by her this time. One thing about it and two things for sure, James isn't going to let anything happen to them. I believe that with my whole heart. I feel like he'll use every last dime to fight for Chandler."

Travis nodded his head and said, "I agree. I know I haven't been around long but I hate they are having to go through this. I hope everything works out for them."

Sharing a common concern for their sister, brother-in-law, and nephew, the brothers bonded.

As they talked, for both Cole and Travis they each spoke with the intentions to see the differences between them as well as the commonalities. The revealed differences and similarities solidified their connection. There was something unique in the way the two were finding ways to relate to one another. It seemed like discovering their differences made their bond work. Almost like they intuitively understood each other.

Cole watched Travis as he talked, he thought, "*He seems to be genuine, like all he really wants is to have a relationship with his family. Dude seems real cool.*"

Knocking on the door, Marissa walked in and said, "I thought we were hungry, what happened?" Tapping her wristwatch, Marissa said, "I'm waiting on pizza and you guys are in here jaw-jacking like people aren't around here starving."

Cole jumped up from the bed and grabbed Marissa by her waist and said, "Well, we can't have you starving now can we? Travis and I were just in here talking and I guess I lost track of time. I'll go and order the pizza now 'lil mama."

Cole turned to Travis and said, "Alright man, I'll come and get you when the pizza and movies get here."

Cole and Marissa walked out of the room, leaving Travis to his reading.

In the kitchen, Cole asked a favor of Marissa, "I'm going to head out to get the movies and the pizza. If you're uncomfortable with doing this, I'll understand but there's something I need you to do while I'm gone."

Filling Marissa in on his request, Cole confirmed with Marissa she was okay, he grabbed his keys and left, saying, "I shouldn't be gone too long but call me if you need me."

CHAPTER 26

Regina's celebration was winding down, Bishop Montgomery had spoken to so many people he'd lost count, only there was one more person waiting to speak with him.

Amongst the crowds of people waiting to have a moment with the good-looking widower, Claude Montgomery, his brother patiently waited for his turn. He was able to blend in because decades separated him from anyone there, and he'd come in very unassuming.

Bishop Montgomery noticed he hadn't seen Cayden-James in a while and decided to go in and check on him.

Inside of his room, Cayden-James was lying on his bed, replaying Ali's number over and over in his head. It seemed to be the only thing that calmed him. Being incarcerated changed him and now being out, he was like a fish out of water. Despite being back home in familiar surroundings, he felt like a foreigner in a strange land.

A knock at the door broke his trance, he answered it by saying, "Yes, come in."

Bishop opened the door and popped his head inside, he said, "Hey son, I'm just checking on you. I haven't seen much of you since we've been back. Have you eaten anything?"

Cayden-James sat up and said, "Nah, there's too many people down there for me. I've been up here chilling, I just kind of wanted to be alone...you know what I mean?"

"Yes, I do." Bishop explained. Turning to leave, before closing the door, Bishop announced, "Things are starting to wind down so come down and get yourself something to eat, okay."

Repositioning his pillow, Cayden-James said, "Alright Bishop, thanks for letting me know."

Walking down the stairs, Bishop took in a deep cleansing breath to prepare himself for the last leg of entertainment before the evening was over.

At the bottom of the stairs, he turned to walk back to the party when he heard, "Well hello there Eugene, long time no see."

Hearing those words chilled him to the bone, his feet stuck to the floor like ice, he couldn't move his body, only his head. Looking behind himself, he matched the voice up with the person he thought spoke them and it was his brother, Claude.

Recognizing his brother's disbelief, Claude walked around to Bishop and patted him on the shoulder and said, "Hey there big brother, trust me, I'm not a ghost. You might want to close your mouth, before you end up catching some flies. Do you remember mother used to tell us that?"

The two brothers laughed as they reflected on their mother's statement.

Offering up his condolence, Claude said, "I know it has been years and I cut all ties with you and the family but when I heard about Regina; I felt like I needed to put that old stuff behind us and come out here to see about you. How are you holding up?"

Staring at his brother, Bishop was at a loss for words, examining the specks of gray hairs to the fine lines in his face, Bishop felt the weight of all of the missed years with his brother. The fullness of the highly emotional feelings engulfed him and he was unashamed as to who might hear him and he began to cry aloud. Bishop stood crying, trying to make sense of the competing feelings of sympathy and joy that he felt from reuniting with his brother resulting from the loss of his wife.

Both brothers stood with changed hearts, hearts opened to the idea of reconciliation. Bishop sobbed and asked, "Have you seen mother? Does she know you are here?"

Claude explained, "I saw her at the funeral but I haven't seen her since I've been here at your home. Hey, I know this is awkward, me showing up like this but I wanted to be here. You and Regina were married for a lot of years so I can only imagine how you must be feeling or going through."

Bishop wiped his eyes and said with a half-hearted laugh, "Regina, Regina, Regina. Tomorrow would've been our thirty-fifth wedding anniversary…she died a week before our anniversary, isn't that something? Regina had a smile that could warm the coldest hearts. You of all people know how she melted mine. It's only been a week and some days I'm unsure of how I'm going to make it but I've already made myself understand that nothing is going to bring her back…she's gone. I begged her not to go you know and she did anyway and just like that, she's gone."

Still standing at the bottom of the stairs, Claude pulled his brother down to the bottom step where they continued to talk and share. Blocking out all the activity around them, Claude tried to comfort his older brother. For hours, they sat and got caught up on over thirty years of conversations.

Over the course of their brotherly exchanges, Bishop asked, "How do you want to go about seeing mother? Are you going to see her before you leave?"

Claude responded saying, "I would love to see her but do you think it might be too much for her in one day?"

Bishop placed one hand over his mouth and then answered, "You have kids that don't know me and I have kids that don't know you. I want you to round up your crew and come back over here with everyone tomorrow and I'll do the same so we can introduce our families. I'll prepare mother, I won't tell her but I'll make sure she isn't too surprised."

Claude smiled then got serious, "Hey listen, I'm sorry I skipped out on the family all those years ago. I let my ego get the best of me and I damaged my relationships with you all because of that and I'm sorry. I hate the reason that brought us together but I want you to know that I want to help you in any way I can. Now, I heard of some rumblings that you might be retiring soon, is that true?"

Bishop shook his head, he confessed to his brother, "I was about to retire and my oldest son was in line to take it over but he has a lot of foolishness going on in his life which will prevent that from happening anytime soon. I have no idea what's going on, nothing seems to make sense to me anymore."

Claude leaned in and asked, "You aren't planning to have service tomorrow are you?"

Answering matter-of-factly, Bishop said, "Oh yeah man, why wouldn't I?"

Objecting, Claude said, "Eugene, I'm not sure that's a good idea. Okay, I can understand not canceling service but I know you aren't preaching, right?"

Bishop looked his brother squarely in the face and said, "And again I say, why wouldn't I?"

"I think you need to give yourself some time Eugene….it's too soon." Claude said.

Blowing out some hot air, Bishop said, "Hey listen, I know you're trying to help and that you mean well but I got this, okay?"

Claude scoffed and said, "Same old Eugene, I see that bull head hasn't softened up much over the years."

The two siblings shared a laugh because they both knew it was true, Bishop Montgomery was as strong willed as he was before.

Claude stood up and said, "Alright man, I'm going to get going, I need to prepare for my message tomorrow and sounds like you do too. Nevertheless, I'll gather my clan together and we'll see you tomorrow after church." Handing Bishop a card, the two brothers hugged and Claude said, "Here's my card, call me if you need anything."

CHAPTER 27

The growl in Travis' stomach made him hop from his bedroom out to the family room where Marissa was seated on the sofa. Hobbling in on crutches, he said, "How much longer you think before Cole gets back with the pizza, I'm so hungry, my stomach is touching my back."

Marissa turned towards Travis and patted the seat next to her on the sofa and invited Travis to come and sit next to her. She said, "I know right, my stomach and I have been talking to each other for the last thirty minutes."

Wanting to be accepted, he sat down. Getting comfortable on the sofa, he propped his leg up on the leather storage ottoman in front of him. Looking at the television, he asked, "So what are we watching?"

"We aren't really watching anything, we're channel surfing. I'm not sure that counts as watching television, what do you think?"

Travis laughed harder than what Marissa's comment required. Watching him, she giggled on the inside. Thinking back on her previous conversation with Cole, she was going to enjoy the next few minutes.

Inching closer to Travis, Marissa asked, "So Travis, it's just us two here, let me ask you this, as the two outsiders of the family, what do you think of the Watsons so far?"

Using broken dialogue, Travis interrupted his own conversation several times with audible pauses. The truth of the matter was, he had opposing emotions regarding them. Since his introduction to the family, he'd formulated strong opinions about each one but for fear of being rejected he kept his judgments to himself. In answering Marissa's question, he simply said, "I think everyone is pretty cool."

Around the Watsons, Travis was mainly quiet because no one usually talked directly to him so he was excited at the opportunity to sit and talk with Marissa. Flipping the question back on her, he said, "What about you, what do you think of them?"

She smirked and said, "Well, I think it's pretty obvious how I feel about Cole but like you, I think everyone is cool."

Changing the subject, Marissa got a little closer and said, "So Travis, who's the lucky lady in your life?"

Marissa's question sent Travis into a coughing spell, he cleared his throat and said, "There is no lucky lady. Everyone can't be like Cole and get a dream girl like you. In all honesty, I haven't really been in the mindset to date since I found out about George. For the time being, I've only been interested with getting to know him."

Marissa lowered her eyes and the tone of her voice and said, "I can understand that but listen, what if you could have a dream girl like me, what would you do then?"

Travis smiled and said, "That would be awesome, so what do you have a sister or something?"

Marissa reached out and touched Travis' hand and said, "No silly, I'm talking about me."

Cutting his eyes towards Marissa, Travis asked, "Has your hunger scrambled your brain? What are you talking about?"

Now seated in close proximity to Travis, Marissa whispered in his ear, "What would you do if you could have me?" The warmth and moistness of her breath caused him to perk up.

With her hand on his leg, she said, "I knew of two brothers who used to share everything and I mean EVERYTHING…you and Cole could be like that. I know you've seen me checking you out, so what do you think?"

Wanting to get up and run, Travis knew that his leg would keep him from sprinting towards the nearest exit. His thoughts raced while he tried to make sense of the situation he now found himself in.

Marissa whispered again, "Don't keep me hanging, so what do you think Travis? Cole and I are here to take care of you right? I could come and check on you after Cole goes to bed and we could get more acquainted if you know what I mean."

Travis grabbed for his crutches and got up, looking at Marissa, he said, "Look, I'm not sure what kind of game you're playing here but you'll have to play it without me. I didn't peg you to be the kind to cheat but do cheaters really have a look? All I know is that Cole is my brother and I'd love to develop a relationship with him. I'm not interested in messing that up…I don't care how fine you are. He's a good guy and even if you don't, I respect his relationship with you."

Marissa giggled uncontrollably and clapped her hands in front of Travis as Cole's keys rustled in the doorway. Granting Travis a standing ovation, Marissa said, "Congratulations, you passed."

Looking from lowered lids, Travis asked, "Passed what?"

Cole walked into the family room and heard Marissa's report and cut in the conversation, "Sounds like you passed the brothers before others test."

With a flushed face, Travis wasn't happy about being the test subject for Cole's allegiance but thrilled he'd won the approval of a member of the Watson family, his younger brother.

Cole smiled and said, "Sit down, I'll get you some pizza, brother."

CHAPTER 28

"How long are you going to go on being sick and not find out what I already know to be true?"

Scarlett reached over Chandler who was lying in between her and James and kissed James. She said, "I don't know what you know to be true but what I know is that I finally feel like our family is safe and secure from the Montgomerys. I still can't believe what happened today.

James returned her kiss with one of his own and said, "Sometimes, good news can be hard to believe but I would proceed with caution where Carson is concerned sweetheart."

"He gave us his word James. Plus not only that, he and Rebekkah are having a baby of their own. Crazy huh, how things can suddenly turn around?"

Looking down at Chandler, James said, "Yes, things have a way of changing which is why as soon as we get back, I'll be speaking with my lawyer to make sure Chandler's adoption is irrevocable."

"You followed the adoption proceedings to a tee, there shouldn't be any reason to be concerned honey." Scarlett said.

"I hear what you're saying but in my line of work, you check, recheck, and check again so I'll be doing that in this instance as well. One can never be too sure." James explained.

Wrinkling her nose with an ugly twist on her mouth, Scarlett said, "I think he's really sorry and meant what he said, you've been telling me all along not to worry and after today, I'm not going to be worrying about him anymore. I'm over it and you should be too. So, before we went down this road, you were talking about something you knew to be true, what might that be Dr. Hartgrove?"

James reached over into a bag on the night stand and plopped a pregnancy test on the bed in front of Scarlett.

With bulging eyes, she screamed a litany of questions, "What is this for? When did you have time to get this? I just not too long ago had a baby, why do you think I need this? There's no way I need that thing. I've been breastfeeding so my cycle hasn't even come back on yet."

James looked at Scarlett and said, "Go take the test and then come back and talk to me."

Protesting, Scarlett said, "I don't need to take this test James."

James said once again, "Go take the test Scarlett."

Chandler giggled underneath them, he was such a happy baby.

Making odd noises in her throat, Scarlett stomped from the bed into the hotel bathroom. Before the allotted two minutes were up, she had an answer. Speaking slowly and stretching out her words, James heard her saying, "What? No way."

Calling from the bed with the baby, James asked, "So, do you want me to come in there or are you going to come back out here?"

A sweating and stunned Scarlett emerged from the bathroom, smirking, she pointed her finger at James and said, "You did this to me."

Showing her a sly grin, he said, "I did and I'd like to do it again and again and again."

Raising her palms, she said, "Now wait a minute, slow down there partner, you're moving a little too fast for me sir...the thought of pregnancy hasn't even crossed my mind, how did you know?"

James secured Chandler on the bed and walked over to Scarlett, he hugged her, kissed her, and thanked her.

Pushing her hair back behind her ear, he said, "I take my role as the priest of my home very seriously. When I committed my life to yours and Chandler's, I accepted the responsibility for becoming the provider and protector you all would need me to be. As your husband, your lover, and your friend, I'm in tuned with everything about you. These last few weeks you've been so distracted so you hadn't been paying attention to your body but I started taking notice in Chee Chee Island when you were the only one that got sick. Plus, I am a doctor you know. Our little family is expanding and I couldn't be happier."

Scarlett's brain scrambled to try and understand what was happening to her in that moment, she said, "I'm pregnant AGAIN. Do you realize we will have two children born in the same year? Is this really what my life has become?"

Sitting down on the bed, James and Scarlett looked at each other and bursted into laughter. James joked around and said, "You wouldn't answer me when I asked you about birth control, I wish I would've known you were relying on breast feeding because as you can see that doesn't work."

Shaking her head in disbelief, Scarlett asked, "Who knew you could get pregnant without a period? Incredible. I didn't know that but I guess you could fill up a library with all of the things I don't know."

James laughed so hard it became soundless, he tried to gather himself so he could explain, he said, "Yes, breastfeeding can delay the return of your period but depending upon your levels of progesterone, you could start ovulating early before your first period returns even while nursing. So, fertility is likely and nursing shouldn't be your only form of control."

They both looked over at Chandler who was entertaining himself on the bed and smiled, James turned to Scarlett and said, "I love you sweetheart."

Placing her hand on his face, Scarlett kissed James and then looked into his eyes and said, "I love you too and guess what, we're having a baby."

The couple settled into the news of their pending arrival and took pleasure in what their love had created.

CHAPTER 29

"How are you holding up?"

Carson stretched his neck and said, "Good as can be expected I guess. I mean, is there a manual somewhere that tells you how you're supposed to feel after on the same day you bury your mother, you find out you have a child that you have no rights to?"

For selfish reasons of her own, Rebekkah rubbed Carson's shoulders and said, "Yeah, that's tough but if it means anything, I think you did the right thing."

"But how do I just give up my son though?" He asked.

Serving him a slice of humble pie, Rebekkah said, "Well you kind of did that on your own when you got rid of his mother to marry me."

Staring down at his feet, he murmured his regret, at the time of his plan, not one time did he consider any potential fallout. He was only focused on taking over the church and marrying Rebekkah. Now, months later, he felt differently but he knew he deserved whatever painful punishments and indictments came as a result of his actions. In his mind, he felt like seeking reconciliation with Scarlett by setting things right with her by allowing Chandler's adoption to go uncontested was the right thing to do. However, in his heart, he wasn't so sure.

Seated at the kitchen table in his home, Carson looked up at Rebekkah and said, "I'm a horrible person, aren't I? It's alright, you can say it; I know it's true."

Picking at her fingers, Rebekkah said, "I wouldn't necessarily call you a horrible person because keep in mind you have something that we all find irresistibly attractive but the truth is, you are something to deal with."

"Is that why you left me Rebekkah? Is that what happened to us, was I the reason you ran away from me?" Carson asked.

Thinking back on everything that happened, Rebekkah sat for a minute and then said, "I'm not exactly sure, for me, all I know is that it just got to be too much and I did what I know how to do best and that's run. I've never been good at dealing with things head on so over the years, I've found ways to run away, whether it's actually running away like I did here or by running away in my mind."

As he and Rebekkah sat and talked, sounds of life were now back in Carson's home. Since she had been gone, the only sounds of communication was small talk with his caretakers. Since she'd been released from the hospital, she'd been staying with him in one of the guest rooms. Having her there made him feel at ease in spite of all that was happening around him.

Pinching the bridge of his nose, Carson asked, "Given all that has happened…are we beyond repair? Are we irretrievably broken Rebekkah, are you still planning to file?"

Rebekkah was a master at understanding emotional complexities of people and how to use them to her advantage for her personal benefit. With Carson's current state, she was now in a position to reconstruct his past behavior and attitudes towards her to suit her needs.

Taking an extended moment to answer, she knew the silence would make Carson feel more guilty.

Before she could answer he said, "You know, I've been doing a lot of thinking trying to figure out why I'm the way that I am and I think it has everything to do with Bishop."

Rebekkah jerked her head back slightly and said, "What are you talking about? You're always talking about how great a father he was and still is and how much he loved your mother. I don't understand."

Carson scoffed and said, "Hmm, yeah he loved my mother but too bad it was all a lie."

Growing concerned, Rebekkah sat up and said, "Carson, what are you talking about? You know what, it has been a long day and a lot has happened. I think you've probably pushed yourself too far and may need to lie down."

Standing to help Carson up from the table, he looked up at Rebekkah and said, "No, sit down...I need to talk about this."

Sitting back down, Rebekkah said, "Okay, I'm listening."

Carson stared at the wall in an attempt to focus his mind, he said, "Yes, I do believe Bishop loved my mother but the thing is he was in love with another woman. Their entire marriage was based upon him having feelings for someone else and he loved my mother through those shared feelings."

Rebekkah ran her fingers through her hair, she asked, "How do you know this?"

Biting at his cheek, Carson explained, "When I was five years old, I saw Bishop with another woman. When I saw them it looked like they were both in pain or something. I now know what that look was all about because when you love someone and can't be with them, it can be painful. I know this because that's how I felt being married to Scarlett but wanting to be with you. Can you believe that, the great, walk the straight line Bishop Montgomery had an affair with another woman and I saw them."

Rebekkah raised her eyebrow and said, "Nothing about that story makes me believe Bishop cheated on Regina. Carson, you were five years old, a number of things could have been happening in the moment you saw them."

Convinced of his memories, Carson said, "You weren't there and the memory of seeing them in his office like that has been seared into my brain from then up until now and I think I made myself believe that if it was okay for Bishop to dibble and dabble, it was certainly okay for me. I oftentimes wondered if my mother knew but she loved Bishop with everything in her, she supported him through thick and thin."

Rebekkah could see that Carson yearned for the return of his mother and that he was certain he knew of his father's indiscretions. She spoke to him in words he needed to hear, she said, "Regina was a remarkable woman, when you met her you could clearly see how much she loved her husband and her children. She will definitely be missed. While I think for a five year old, you may have misinterpreted what you saw but I'm glad you are having a chance to get it out and talk about it."

Carson grabbed Rebekkah's hand and said, "I'm glad you're here. You're the only person I've ever shared that with and I do think talking about has helped me to feel better in some small way. I wanted to tell you that to give you a little insight into me and why I probably have so many issues. Rebekkah, I want to do things differently, with us having a baby, give me a chance to make things right between us. I need you, stay with me tonight...in our room."

The diagnosis of leukemia may have made him weak on some days but his desire was still strong, that part of him had not declined.

Seizing the moment, Rebekkah stood up and walked over to him and said, "We're having a baby and I'm here tonight, that's all I know right now. I'm not making you any promises Carson, let's just take one day at a time.

Carson pulled her close and kissed her, he remembered her touch and the hold she had upon him; he then took her by the hand and led her upstairs.

CHAPTER 30

"Welcome home."

Travis, Cole, and Marissa stood at the door as the Watson/Hartgrove clan arrived back at George and Minta's house. With the good news that Carson wasn't going to be a problem for James and Scarlett, they decided to decorate the house and celebrate the good news. Cole also thought it would be a great time to celebrate his accomplishments with Marissa as well.

Once inside, everyone hugged and greeted each other, George was happy to see the smiles that Travis and Cole wore on their faces. He asked Travis, "So they took good care of you huh?"

Travis caught the eye of both Cole and Marissa and they all laughed as he said, "Uh yeah, they sure did."

George smiled and said, "Oh so you guys have insider jokes now I see, okay, okay. So you guys had a good weekend then?"

Cole said, "Yes, we did dad, I'm glad we came up. It gave me a chance to get to know my brother a little better."

Hearing the word brother, Scarlett and Minta turned their heads towards the conversation, interested to witness the burgeoning bond between the two brothers.

Minta turned to get in on the conversation but was distracted by Marissa reaching up in a cabinet to grab a bowl.

Without thinking, Minta blurted out, "Marissa, are you pregnant?"

Stepping down from the step stool, Marissa dropped the glass bowl in response to Minta's allegation.

That shattered glass got everyone's attention as they turned and saw a flush faced Marissa.

Cole marched over to Marissa and said, "What's wrong love?"

Marissa whispered to Cole, "She just asked me if I'm pregnant."

With all eyes on them, Cole looked at his family smiling and said, "Well, we wanted to celebrate Scarlett and James' good news but we also thought today would be a good day to share and celebrate some good news of our own. We wanted to tell you guys during the baby shower weekend but we all know what happened then." Looking over at Travis, Cole said, "Sorry bro, no offense."

Travis nodded and said, "None taken brother."

Cole continued, "With everything going on, it never seemed like the right time to tell you guys but pretty soon our surprise is going to be telling on us. So family, my wife and I are going to be having a baby."

Minta shouted out, "Wife? Pregnant? What?"

Scarlett and James smiled at each other and she chimed in and said, "Not to steal your moment but you're right, a lot has been going on so it does make it hard to get news out so with that being said, congratulations you two, we're having one too."

The Hartgroves jumped up and down, Derrick and Rena said, "Wow, hearing that news makes our decision to stick around a little longer make even more sense. We're going to be hanging around in Jordan for a while."

Everyone cheered and clapped and hugged and congratulated the two couples, all except Minta.

Standing in the middle of the kitchen, she shouted and said, "Wait. Stop it, right now…everybody just wait one minute. Cole, how are you married and we don't know that, how long have you two been married?"

Marissa's worst nightmare had come true, she had feared Minta's reaction and Minta wasn't disappointing, she was being overly dramatic.

Cole walked up to Minta and kissed her on the cheek saying, "My wife and I have been married for about four months now. This isn't information I wanted to share over the phone mom. We've been so busy with school and so much was going on with Scarlett and I wanted you all to take care of her as much as possible. One day I decided I no longer wanted to just be Marissa's boyfriend that I wanted to be her husband so I called her dad, made a quick trip to see him to ask for her hand and he gave me his blessing. Soon after getting married, we got pregnant."

Shaking her head and under her breath, Minta said, "My God, my God…the whore of Babylon is present in my house."

George swung around and shouted, "Minta…how dare you."

Marissa broke down and started crying, Cole yelled at his mother, "This is my wife and the mother of my child, why would you say such a thing?"

Minta spewed out her reasoning, "Cole, you are a successful young man with a bright future, women are always on the lookout for men with money, power, and influence and you have that. Can't you see what this is? Listen, you are my son and I only want what's best for you. If things were on the up and up y'all would have been upfront with us instead of hiding it."

Rena observed Minta's outbursts and thought, "Is this how Christians are supposed to behave? *I thought she'd be happy to be welcoming another grandchild. I know I am. I guess what they say about mothers and sons is true but I didn't act like this with James and Scarlett."*

Pulling at his collar, George was completely let down by Minta, he couldn't believe what she'd said. He knew how strongly she felt about their children and that ultimately the surprise of the information was what had her upset but he felt like this time, she had gone too far.

Cole stepped up to his mother and said, "Nobody hid anything, things have been crazy around here, to say the least." Defending his wife's honor he said, "Marissa is a highly educated woman currently studying for a specialty, she's successful in her own right." Providing her with his available options, he said, "If you ever want to see me or your grandchild ever in life, you'd better apologize to my wife and make things right with her." Without flinching, Cole said through clenched teeth, "Do it now or we're out of here."

Minta stood tapping her foot with her arms crossed and turned her head.

Cole grabbed Marissa by the hand and walked out of the house.

George ran out behind them.

CHAPTER 31

Despite carrying on service at Wondrous Works, the mood inside the sanctuary was toned-down significantly and the attendance was in short supply. Canceling the service was probably the better idea but Bishop felt the need to continue on as usual, he felt like Regina would have wanted him to keep going.

As he stood on the platform, he turned to do his traditional acknowledgement of his family but the chairs were all empty. No one was there but the one empty seat that gripped his heart was Regina's. It was their anniversary and he had planned to serenade her during the service and have her gift delivered on the stage. The realization that he would never get to honor her in a service overwhelmed him. Yes, they were going through a rough patch but he missed her something terrible. Trying to put the best foot forward, he hadn't given himself anytime to grieve.

Standing in front of his congregation, he opened his mouth to speak but nothing came out. He had difficulty forming responses. His armor bearer approached him but he waved him off.

Touching his temple he closed his eyes and tried it again, yet instead of words, he let out an uncontrollable sob.

Hovering over the podium, Deacon Bob Thomas, head of the Trustee board came and ushered him off of the platform and into his office.

Sitting him down, Bob said, "You can't keep this up Bishop. I think you should take some time off and focus on healing from this tragedy. The church will understand. As head of your trustee board, you should know that the other board members and I have begun the process in vetting other pastoral candidates."

Bishop quickly settled himself and asked, "Why would you all decide to do that? I haven't asked you to do that."

Bob said, "You placed me in this position to make sure the church runs smoothly and to be honest sir, the ship needs some steering."

Bishop said, "But other pastoral candidates don't sound like members of the Montgomery family."

"And maybe that's a good thing." Bob said.

Bishop stood up and said, "Now hold on a minute Bob, need I remind you this is my family's church. It was founded by Montgomerys and it will continue to be pastored by Montgomerys. Do you understand me? Now, I realize that I may need to take a little break but Bob, listen to me, don't try and use my family's issues as an excuse for a hostile takeover."

Bob sat next to Bishop and took a long pause before responding, when he did, he said, "My wife has a friend, her family owns a quaint bed and breakfast inn over in the next county. They pride themselves on offering the utmost privacy to their guests. It's one of the hidden gems here in Vino, not many people know about it and it's done like that on purpose, it's very exclusive. I'm going to place a call and see about getting you set up there for as long as you feel you need to be there."

Without much resistance, Bishop said, "Alright Bob, but listen, my brother is supposed to be bringing his family over today. Let me meet up with them and I'll leave this evening."

Bob called his wife, Hazel who made the arrangements at the inn, she made the reservation for an open-ended departure date.

Placing his hand on Bishop's shoulder, Bob said, "You're all set my friend, take as much time as you need. Don't worry about anything here, Wondrous Works will be fine and over time, you will be too."

Rubbing his head, Bishop said, "Thank you and I hope you're right...I so hope you're right Bob."

Bob Thomas returned in the service, the praise and worship leaders took over the service by singing when their Bishop left. He walked up to podium and announced that today's service as well as Wednesday night's service would be cancelled.

CHAPTER 32

Cayden-James took out his phone, he flipped it over like playing a game of heads or tails. Being back home hadn't felt like what he'd imagined, he was having a hard time finding his footing. He'd been spending a lot of time in his room, thinking a lot about what his future and what was next for him.

Sitting at his computer, he logged onto his old securities account. As a teenager, he'd taken an interest in day trading but because of his age, he had only been able to paper trade and perform online trade simulations. Based on his crimes, he was prohibited from having anything to do with Bitcoins but no one said anything about the stock market.

The night before he'd placed a stop loss order on a stock he'd been monitoring, based on his account balance, he still had it. While prison had changed him, his approach to investing had not.

When his phone landed on heads, he made a transfer of funds and made a phone call.

On the other end, Ali answered.

Stumbling over his words, Cayden-James said, "Um, hi...may I speak to -."

Having to actually say her name caused him to freeze, he panicked and hung up the phone.

Beating himself in the head, he cringed at his scaredy-cat behavior, he knew he wasn't a punk so why was he so nervous.

Trying not to overthink it, he dialed her right back, "Yeah um, I'm sorry…I think my phone dropped the call but I'm Cayden-James and I'm trying to reach Ali Joyner."

Chuckling a little, Ali said, "This is she and I know who you are."

Cayden-James steadied his sea legs and said, "Oh so you know who I am huh?" Joking around, he said, "I guess I made a wonderful impression on you."

Smiling through the phone, Ali remarked, "Now, I wouldn't say all of that."

"Of course not." Cayden-James replied.

Turning the conversation serious for a moment, Ali said, "I knew you were going to get out but before I bust your chops about that, I'd like to say I heard the news about your mother and I'm sorry for you loss. I've lost a parent before but I can't say I know how you feel, especially by you having lost your mother."

Cayden-James nodded and thanked Ali, he said, "Yeah, that's part of the reason I called you. I know how you feel about what I've done and about me getting out early but I want to do something about it. I've been doing a lot of thinking since I've been out and I've been trying to figure out a lot of things. I wanted to find a way to honor my mother's life and all that she stood for. As a result, I've created the Regina Montgomery Scholarship Fund and I know who the first recipient should be."

"Who is it?" Asked Ali.

Cayden-James laughed and said, "Duh, why you of course. You mentioned you were studying psychology in school before you had to drop out and I have an idea I want to pursue but I need your help. I have an offer for you if you're interested."

Intrigued, Ali said, "I'm listening."

Placing the call on speaker, he sat back at his computer and pulled a document he'd been working on. Clicking through the pages he said, "Okay so here's what I'm offering. I have an idea called Trader Traits™, essentially, it is a program whereby I will create a trading platform based on people's personalities. Based on a questionnaire, the information will assess and evaluate a person's affinity towards investing and will offer trades based upon their level of risk. As you can see, based on what I'm trying to do, I will need your help and expertise."

"You could hire anyone to help you do that part, I'm not even done with school yet so why me?" She asked.

Cayden-James threw his head back and said, "You make an excellent point and might think this is just about you but this helps me out as well. When you came to see me, you put a face to all of my victims. You made me face the reality of what I'd done and even though I've paid my debt to society, I want to do more and you are my motivation."

Ali asked, "So what are the conditions of this offer? What would I need to do?"

"Move out here to California." He said quickly.

"Why?" She questioned.

Prior to calling Ali, Cayden-James had gone through a list of possible objections she might have so he had a number of answers for her to overcome any objections she might have. He switched ears on his phone and said, "Well, my father sits on the board of the university here and I've already spoken with him and he's going to fast track you through the admissions department. Not only that I think I can get the information I need from you easier if you live here instead of having to wait and do video chats, conference calls, or emails. Don't worry, your scholarship will include full tuition, room and board, books, and you'll even receive a monthly stipend."

Ali spoke up and said, "Let me think about it and I'll get back with you."

She thought to herself, "*This is a no-brainer but I don't want to seem too eager to take him up on his offer so I'll make him sweat a little bit.*"

Cayden-James pursed his lips together and thought, "*What is there to think about,*" but instead he said, "Okay, well, when can I expect to hear from you?"

Trying to keep her smile from coming through the phone, she said, "Uh, give me a day or two and I'll call you back. Is this a good number to call you on?"

Shutting down his computer he said, "Yes, you can call me on this number anytime. And Ali, I hope to hear from you real soon."

CHAPTER 33

Mother Montgomery stood at the window, after returning home from service, Bishop filled her in and prepped her for what was about to take place. She had decided she wasn't going to move from that spot until she laid eyes on her baby boy.

For the first time, Cayden-James was downstairs without having been called, he was smiling and laughing, he walked in and said, "You can at least sit down and wait on them, can't you grandma?"

Waving him off, she said, "Now, I'm glad to see you up and out of that room but you let me be. When I want to sit down, I'll sit down, right now, I want to stand up."

She didn't have to stand much longer because Claude and his caravan was pulling onto the property.

Mother Montgomery clasped her hands across her chest and said, "They're here."

Thirty-five years of distance and vastness of time and space was now filled with warmth and love. The two Montgomery brothers brought their families together with their mother in the middle. Grandchildren and great grandchildren met their grandmother and nieces and nephews were introduced while cousins became acquainted.

Regina never got a chance to meet Claude's wife, Lillian and Bishop knew instantly that the two would have gotten along beautifully.

Bishop kept the tent from Regina's celebration so most of the activity was taking place outside. During the dinner, everyone was seated around the table with Mother Montgomery at the head of the table. Her heart was filled with joy, she sat tapping her feet saying, "Thank you Lord, I have all of my children here with me. This is one of the greatest days of my life."

After dinner, the large group dispersed into several areas around the house.

Bishop thought it would be a good idea to play a few games in an effort to continue getting acquainted.

On the way into the family room, Cherie pulled Carson aside and asked to speak with him privately.

Walking into the study, he turned to her and said, "What's up Cherie? What's going on with you?"

Rocking slightly in the chair, Cherie said, "I need to talk to you about something. I need your help but I need you to promise me you'll keep this between us."

Cupping his elbow with one hand, Carson tapped his lips with the other hand saying, "Okay, I'm listening."

Cherie said, "As you know, I've just gotten back from being on tour and from what I understand there's a tape out there."

Edging closer he said, "What kind of tape?"

Being the latest black sheep of the family and resident bad boy, Cherie felt comfortable speaking to Carson about her troubles. She felt it would be far easier to talk to him than any of the others. Crossing her legs, she said, "Supposedly there's a video of me with some people doing some things we wouldn't be proud of it if it got out."

Carson blew out a deep breath and asked, "How bad is it?"

Cherie blew out a deeper breath, she replied, "It's really bad…really, really, bad." Starting to tear up she said, "Carson, I can't afford for this video to get out, it could ruin my career, my ministry."

"So what's the deal, is someone trying to blackmail you with it or what? Why hasn't it been leaked yet?" He asked.

Cherie stood up and paced the floor, "I'm not sure, I've been waiting to hear from my manager since I've been here but I haven't heard anything and I can't get in touch with him. He told me he was going to try squash it before things got out of hand but I'm not sure. This could really hurt the family and I feel horrible, if this gets out, Auntiemama Regina will roll over in her grave a hundred times in one minute."

Cherie was young and immature, she was blessed with a beautiful voice and wanted to try her hand at a singing career but she wanted to go the secular route and Regina was totally against that. With reservations, Cherie did give into Regina's request since Regina did call in a few favors to get Cherie's career up and going.

Unfortunately, Cherie was singing songs for the Lord but not living for Him. She used her platform as a gospel singer to pursue better entertainment opportunities. She learned early on that even in Christian entertainment circles, darkness was available to those who played around with the light. The first time she went out on the road, she arrived at a venue and the organizers asked her what she wanted in her dressing room, suggesting the standard items, she was asked about drugs, sex, and alcoholic choices.

Carson scratched the side of his face and said, "I guess this is what mother feared for you. Many times she would quote 1 John 2:16[7] and say, I pray for Cherie all the time while she's out there on the road. She'd say, I don't want her getting caught up in

---

[7] **1 John 2:16**: "For all that is in the world, the lust of the flesh, and the lust of the eyes, and the pride of life, is not of the Father, but is of the world."

all that fast living. I can hear her now saying, I hope Cherie doesn't get pulled into the lust of the flesh, eyes, and pride of life."

Hearing Regina's concern for her made Cherie cry even more, she said, "I know it. She'd call me and tell me the same thing but I guess my desire to have fun and quest for fame and money, I got sidetracked for what was really important and that's my soul. This situation with this tape and aunt Regina's death has got me to thinking about that."

Carson stood up and sat on the edge of the desk, he looked at Cherie and said, "Well, one thing about it and two things for sure, shaming the family and finding yourself in heavy situations like this will cause you to grow up and mature, real fast. Take it from me, I know. So what do you want me to do?"

Cherie blew her nose and said, "I mean, what would you do if you were me? I know you've had some experience with the crisis management people here at the church so do you think you could pose the situation to them and see what they might recommend? The greatest outcome I could hope for is that somehow that video gets destroyed."

Carson inquired deeper, "Now you say there are some other people involved, how many people are in the video and who has the recording?"

Cherie lowered her head and said, "One of the drummers has it; he mentioned to my manager that he was in possession of it."

Carson took out a sticky note and asked, "What's the drummer's name?"

"His name is Johnson Blue." Cherie replied.

Placing the note in his pocket, Carson walked around towards Cherie and opened his arms up to her, comforting her he said, "Don't worry about it, I'll look into this for you. I'll take care of it."

"What are you going to do?" She asked.

Carson assured Cherie by saying, "Don't you trouble yourself with the details, just think about how you are going to start turning things around in your life."

CHAPTER 34

Inside the Watson home, everyone sat around the table discussing ALL of the news that had come out that day, starting with Cole and Marissa to James and Scarlett's pregnancy announcement to Rena and Derrick choosing to stick around for a while all the way to Minta's ugly display of her disapproval.

George had followed Cole and Marissa outside and decided to take them for a ride to cool things down in the home. He texted Minta and practically demanded her to get herself together and be prepared to make an apology and ask for forgiveness when they returned.

Up in her bedroom, ashamed of her behavior, Minta prayed and cried out to God, asking him to show her why she responded in such a way. As she sat on her bed, a fleeting thought crossed her mind.

In her mind she was taken back to the time when Cole was a baby. At the time, the family employed a housekeeper by the name of Adelaide. Having a newborn and a toddler, Minta was beyond exhausted but she tried to be supermom and do things all on her own while George worked. Scarlett had been a dream as a baby but Cole was colicky. Noticing Minta's state of tiredness, Adelaide offered to watch the children for a while so she could get some rest. Unable to quiet and calm the fussy baby, Adelaide made a decision to medicate an ornery Cole.

Refreshed from her nap, Minta lost complete control when she found her baby unresponsive. Trying with all of her might, she tried everything she could to wake Cole but nothing worked. As a young mother she freaked out and ran to Adelaide and questioned her only to find out what she'd done. With her words, Minta ripped her housekeeper into shreds as she frantically filled Cole's tub with cold water. Lowering him into the cold water woke him up and he began crying all over again. In that moment, Minta fired Adelaide. When George asked why, she told him she could handle the kids and the house and that a housekeeper was no longer needed in their home. On that day, she vowed to Cole that she would never let anything happen to him and that she'd always be around to protect him.

Connecting with the root cause of her outburst, Minta asked the Lord to remove the residue from that moment from her spirit and she asked the Lord for the right words to say to everyone.

Downstairs, George had walked in with Cole and Marissa as Minta made it downstairs to meet them.

Standing in the middle of the kitchen she asked for everyone's attention.

A disgraced Minta stood looking down at her feet as she couldn't meet anyone's eyes at that time. Pulling her arms towards her core she said, "I have totally and completely embarrassed myself in here today. I have acted so far outside of my character and I'm so ashamed. I first want to say I'm sorry to everyone in here." Walking up to Marissa, she grabbed her hand and said, "I'm so very sorry for what I said. I really didn't mean it, there really isn't any excuse for what I did but I was upset and I let that get the best of me. I know it may take some time but I'm sure hoping you'll find it in your heart to forgive me."

Marissa stood squinting her eyes, unsure as to how to respond to her new mother-in-law, she didn't say anything she just nodded.

Minta reached in for a hug and Marissa returned it with a half-hearted one.

Moving onto Cole she said, "Thank you for standing up to me today. You showed me how much you really care for this young lady and if you can put me in my place like that you must really love her. I'm sorry and I hope you can forgive me son."

With a stiff neck, Cole said, "If Marissa's okay, then I'm okay."

Minta walked over to Travis and said, "I'm sorry Travis…not just for today but for every day since you've been around. You hadn't done anything to me and yet I've been treating you like you have. I promise that you have my word that I'm going to do my best to do better by you in the days ahead. I too hope you can find it in your heart to forgive me."

Happy to be hearing Minta's words, Travis hopped up on his good leg and gave Minta a big hug and kiss on the cheek.

Standing next to Rena and Derrick, she said, "I can only imagine what you two must be thinking of me; I invite you into my home and I then I act like this. I hope you will still consider staying here with us while you find something more permanent. It looks like I'm going to need more grandmother support with all of these babies coming on the scene."

Rena and Derrick accepted Minta's apology and gave her a hug.

Scarlett looked at her mother and said, "No need to apologize, we all know you are a crazy woman, all is forgiven. James and Scarlett placed their arms around Minta and hugged her.

The last man standing was George. He'd watched Minta humble herself and go down the line apologizing to everyone. She walked up to him and placed her arms around his waist. She looked up at him and said, "There is no other man that could love me like you do. Through all of the craziness and ups and downs, you're always here for me and I thank you. I'm so sorry honey and I appreciate you for setting me straight, you forced me to take a look at myself and I did." Reaching up for a kiss, George reciprocated and kissed her. She said, "I love you George."

He held her close and said, "I love you too Minta."

Calling everyone back into the kitchen, Minta announced, "In an effort to make up for my despicable behavior today, I've made arrangements for this evening. I hope you all aren't too mad at me and will join me at the club for a dinner reception to officially welcome Marissa and Travis into our family. Right now as I speak, the staff up at the club are preparing a wonderful celebration for us."

Walking over to Marissa, Minta grabbed both of Marissa's hands and said, "I've called in a favor to my favorite boutique and they are going to bring over a few things for you to try on, hopefully you'll find something in there you'll like and care wear for tonight." Turning and looking at Cole and Travis she said, "They carry men's clothes as well and will be bringing some things for you guys as well."

Marissa accepted Minta's gesture of amnesty.

The mood was changing in the room as Minta was making recompense for her transgressions.

Minta asked to speak to Rena, she pulled her aside and said, "I know I've apologized but I want you to know that I'm so very sorry that you saw me act like that. I just lost it for a moment, I've always heard that it is different between mothers and sons but I never realized it until today. Nevertheless, as a woman who claims to love the Lord, my conduct didn't reflect that today and I hope that doesn't make you think differently of me. You know, sometimes I haven't to be reminded that if I'm going to talk the talk then I need to also walk the walk."

Rena grabbed Minta's hand and said, "When I had James, when I laid eyes on him for the first time, I fell in love so I understand the bond a mother has with her son. I want you to know that I really appreciate you for coming and talking to me. You immediately let us know that you were a Christian, quoting your scriptures and everything. For me, you are the only bible I've ever seen, which means the same for others you come in contact with. I will say this, since we've been around you guys, I feel like there is something tugging at me and I'm not sure what it is but I am interested in finding out more about it."

Tears welled up on Minta, Rena's words touched her deeply, causing her to realize that her witness for the Lord was still important. She thanked Rena, hugged her and said, "I'll be praying for you, I pray as you seek, you will find my sister, now let's get ready to have some fun and enjoy our children."

CHAPTER 35

The Montgomery family reunion had been a huge success, new family members were exchanging contact information and befriending one another on social media sites.

The evening was coming to a close when Christian stood in the middle of the room and asked for Courtney to join him.

Christian grabbed Courtney's hand and took in a deep breath, he said, "I'm glad that I got a chance to meet you all and get acquainted but this maybe the last time for a while before I get to see any of you again."

Bishop put his cup down and asked, "What are you talking about son?"

Christian looked at Courtney and said, "We're leaving town…we're moving."

"Why?" Bishop asked.

"Why not?" Christian countered.

Bishop stood up and said, "What's this all about Christian? I need you here and I definitely need you at the church."

Christian shook his head and said, "That's just it Bishop. I can't do this church thing anymore; I can't stay here any longer. I feel like if I stay here I'll die."

Mother Montgomery spoke up and said, "What do you mean you can't do this church thing anymore?"

He'd tried to make a peaceful announcement but they were pushing him, he said, "This whole church life killed my mother. Living this life has done nothing but take from me. You'd think growing up in the church under such a powerful man of God, we would have learned something in all of the Sunday school classes we were forced to go to but I'm not sure we learned a thing. Cayden-James is a convicted felon, Carson should be one, Cherie is on her way to being on America's Funniest Videos or maybe not…yeah, I heard overheard your conversation with Carson, and I'm all screwed up in the head. Thanks Wondrous Works, you've really done a work in my life."

Bishop Montgomery looked at Cherie and Carson and asked, "Do I even want to know what he's referring to?"

They both shook their heads no and left the room. Bishop spoke softly, "C'mon now Christian. Don't you think you're being a little unfair? You act as if I chose this life. I didn't God chose this life for me; I was called to pastor."

Christian shot back and said, "Yeah but I wasn't. Do I have to suffer at the hands of your calling? I'm tired of this…you know what, I didn't grow up like all my friends that grew up with their dads. I didn't grow up with a dad, I grew up with a Bishop."

Family members starting filing out of the room as the conversation continued to escalate. Those who remained, could identify with Christian even if they would never admit it.

Courtney stood with tears streaming down her face.

Mother Montgomery asked her, "Courtney honey, do you feel the same way? How do you feel about leaving?"

Courtney looked at Mother Montgomery and said, "He's my husband, I have to go where he goes right? I think it was you that warned me to be careful what I ask for."

Christian announced to the remaining, "I've accepted a job at a new law firm where I'll be in a leadership position and Courtney is considering starting her own firm. Maybe one day, she'll let me work for her."

Cayden-James walked up to his brother and said, "So you help get me out and you're just going to leave me hanging out here like that?"

Christian shook his head and said, "I'm sorry little brother but I can't do it; I can't stay here anymore. The time has come for me to move on, we leave in a week.

Upset at his brother's news, the buzz in his pocket soon changed his outlook. Retrieving the phone from his pocket, he read a message from Ali that read: "**Where do I sign up for the Regina Montgomery Scholarship Fund?**"

CHAPTER 36

Standing outside of The Bolts, the bed and breakfast, Bob set up for him, Bishop let out a deep sigh thinking of how he would have loved to be going to a bed and breakfast to celebrate his anniversary but instead he was there alone, to grieve.

The front desk manager, Angela greeted him warmly and checked him in under the alias, Thomas Peterson, all Bob's doing. Unbeknownst to him the front desk manager was Delores Bolton's niece. To her, he was a regular guest staying at her family's inn.

Angela oriented him to the property and the itinerary. She made sure he was safe and secured in his room as she checked in on some of the other guests.

Inside of his room, Bishop plopped down on the bed, stretching out completely over the entire bed. In the peacefulness and tranquility of his room, he laid still without saying a word. In that moment he realized how he started taking notice to details he never would have before such as the tick tock of the clock on the wall. Looking up in the ceiling, he noticed the hairline cracks in the ceiling.

For the first time since Regina's death, Bishop found himself with nothing to do, there was no funeral to plan, no suit to pick out for burial, no insurance and bank business to attend to, and no church affairs to worry about. The alone time frightened him, he reached in his bag and pulled out Regina's favorite broach, it was one she cherished from her mother. Holding it close, he now found comfort in it. All week he'd fought against questioning God but being alone, he couldn't seem to help wonder, why did He have to take her and why now. Forcing his mind not to make a demand for an answer of mistrusting God's timing but if truth be told, he felt a sense of betrayal that rocked his mind to its very core…he didn't understand.

Feeling broken inside, he moved from the bed and over to the table and sat in one of the chairs, he opened his bible to try and escape to see if that would ease his troubled soul but that didn't work.

He stared down at his hands and thought back to the prayer Claude prayed over the family before leaving his home, Claude had prayed, "Lord, you know our sorrow better than we know it ourselves. You know how easy it is for our worried souls to get caught up with the inconvenient cares of this world. We do pray Father that whatever you do bring us to, we will receive it with humble hearts and You'll bring us through with renewed strength. Lord, heal us of our sorrow, in Jesus' name. Amen."

Thinking back on the prayer, the words did provide him with some level of comfort however, it was short lived. The pain was weighing on him more than the consolations. His longings were so intense they manifested themselves in aches and anguish. He wanted the pain to stop but he didn't have a clue as to how to make that happen.

Being on his own, he would sometimes catch himself having bouts of uncontrollable crying fits while other times he now talked to himself. Dredging up memories from their last few months, the problems they were having and tried to understand what led them there.

He opened the private, mini snack and beverage bar. For the first time in his fifty-nine years, he heard the whispers from the Whiskey, he heard the call of the Cognac, the bid from the Bourbon appealed to him and he answered them all.

Popping their tops he poured the smooth, yet harsh liquids in the glass and gulped them down his throat. In that moment, he didn't accept the grace exchange available to him for his grief and heartache, in his weakness, he took matters into his own hands

Turning on his tablet, he pulled up a playlist he'd created before leaving home. He put on "Take My Hand," a rendition of "Precious Lord" on repeat and drank himself to sleep.

In his clothes, in his drunken stupor, in his agony, he slept in the chair all night.

CHAPTER 37

Loosening his belt, Carson crawled onto his bed and kissed Rebekkah on the cheek saying, "Boy, what a day huh? These last two weeks have been filled with peaks and valleys. I don't know how we are making it through but I guess the scripture is true that says He won't put more on you than you can bear. I have to say we must be pretty strong because we've been bearing a lot here lately."

Rebekkah ran her fingers through Carson's thinning hair, his curls were starting to grow back. She kissed him in the top of his head and said, "Yes, you guys are strong which makes me happy that our baby is going to have that same resilient spirit."

Carson reached over and rubbed Rebekkah's stomach, he repositioned his body so he could speak directly towards her belly and said, "Hey in there, how are you doing in there today? Your mommy and daddy are just out here hanging out talking and thinking about you. Be good in there okay."

Rebekkah smiled as she listened to Carson. She looked at him and said, "So, I've been dying to ask you, what's going on with Cherie and what do you think of Christian and Courtney leaving town?"

Tapping his fingers against his forehead, Carson said, "Oh, um, Cherie, no need to concern yourself there and I don't have much to say about Courtney and Christian. I mean, I think this entire situation has all of us thinking about what's next for our lives. Mother was the glue, she was the nucleus of our family and without her it's like can the body still function without the heartbeat? I know for me and I'm sure we are all trying to figure out where do we go from here. Everyone grieves differently and so we all will have varying ways to deal and cope and I guess the way he's choosing to deal with his is to leave. It's unfortunate because I'm very concerned about Bishop and even Grandma Montgomery. However, with the things going on in my own life I need to be focusing on my health and getting better so I can be a better man for you and our child."

Rebekkah asked a question she already knew the answer saying, "So are you saying me and this baby means more to you than your own life?"

Carson looked up at Rebekkah and said, "What I'm saying is that you and this baby have given me a second chance at life and I want to make the best of it. The cycle of life is something else. My mother dies but I find out we're having a baby and also that there's a baby out there with my DNA. It's crazy but there comes a time when you have to absolutely grow up and face the music and if these last few weeks haven't taught me anything, I've come to the realization that I have a lot of atoning to do and I want to change the tide and start sowing some seeds of goodwill instead of living how I had been. There comes a time when you know better, you should try and do better."

Cocking her head to the side, Rebekkah was impressed, time had brought about a change and Carson's life lessons had indeed taught him something. She grabbed his face up in both of her hands and kissed him on his lips and said, "It makes me very happy to hear you say that. In fact, I'm very impressed by you right now."

Tossing her a suggestive smile and inching closer, he said, "How impressed are you?"

The Big Bonanza

Rebekkah looked him up and down and licked her lips.
She knew her to control him, her flirtation made him feel important
and attractive. She leaned in to kiss him and stopped shy of his
lips and breathed deeply, she was driving him crazy and he was
eating up every bit of it. She whispered, "Let me use the restroom,
I want to freshen up a little and I'll be right back."

"Now don't be gone too long Rebekkah, I'm ready to make
an even bigger impression on you." He joked.

Inside the bathroom, Carson heard the shower start, he
leaned back on the pillows and smiled as he was grateful to have
Rebekkah back home and especially during his time of
bereavement.

With the shower running, she couldn't hear that her phone
was ringing but Carson could. The phone displayed a picture of
Godfrey with his corresponding phone number on the screen.

By Rebekkah not answering, Godfrey decided to leave a
text message that Carson took the liberty to read: "**I'm going
crazy over here, call me.**"

Hearing the water shut off, Carson sent a text message of
his own, he pulled up Karen's number, his nurse and sent her the
following message: "**Hey, is it possible to get a DNA test during
pregnancy?**"

Karen quickly responded: "**Yes, very simple and 99%
accurate.**"

Carson replied: "**How's it done?**"

Karen came back with: "**Blood from mom, cheek swab
from dad.**"

Carson asked: "**How long before you get the results?**"

Karen answered: "**Around 5-7 business days.**"

Carson inquired: "**Can you fast track it?**"

Karen responded: "**I'll have to check.**"

Rebekkah walked out of the bathroom wrapped in a body towel, Carson sent one last text before she dropped it to the floor.

Carson: **"Let's do this tomorrow."**

Karen: **"Okay."**

Rebekkah grabbed Carson's phone from his hand and tossed on the night stand by the bed. She pulled him close and they fell back on the bed. It was like old times, the two spent a glorious night together.

CHAPTER 38

Arriving at the baggage claim, Delores placed her bags on a cart and walked over to the rental car counter to pick up her car.

The closer she got to the counter, her hands warmed up and got sweaty. The quiver in her stomach and the prickly feeling on her scalp made her realize she needed to find a way to calm her restless mind and body. She stopped for a moment and took in a deep, cleansing breath and thought, *"It shouldn't be this hard, I'm here in my hometown, what's the big deal?"*

From the last conversation that Dottie and Delores had, Dottie started an all-out campaign, "Operation Come Home" to get Delores into town. Dottie called Delores' children and got them on board, she called Delores' pastor and anyone else she could think of that could help convince Delores to come home for a visit.

At the counter, the associate made the car rental process seamless, she was in and out with no problems at all.

Riding through town, Delores started to pay attention to all of the changes and development that had taken place in Vino. She hadn't been home in over thirty-five years and in that time, a lot had changed. The more she drove and took in the sights, the more at ease she became. So much so, she decided to go into town and see what was different there before heading to see her sister.

In a leisurely stroll down the cobblestone streets throughout downtown, Delores smiled as she did a little window shopping.

Not one time had she ever regretted leaving, she'd always felt like leaving Vino was for the best. In leaving, she met and married Charles and they'd shared a beautiful life together, a life that was safe and secure. Nevertheless, walking through her hometown she came to the conclusion that it felt good to be home. As a child, she loved growing up in Vino and being back, the charm of Vino had captured her heart again.

Crossing over to the other side of the street, she was excited to look inside and see the next set of shops.

As she passed the old shoe store where the family used to get their shoes from which was now a realtor's office, she walked upon a restaurant with outdoor seating.

Having been gone for so long, not one time did it cross her mind that anyone would recognize her…but someone did.

Seated outside having lunch with her newly introduced daughter-in-law, Mother Montgomery and Lillian were getting acquainted over soup and salad.

Mother Montgomery spotted Delores and thought back to the meetings, she and her husband had with her many years ago.

Touching Lillian on the hand, Mother Montgomery asked, "Excuse me dear, do you mind, I see someone I'd like to speak to."

None the wiser, Lillian smiled and said, "Oh no, go ahead, I'll be right here."

Easing her way from the table, Mother Montgomery moseyed her way outside of the restaurant and quickly prepped herself in anticipation for what she might say.

In complete oblivion, Delores wandered along absorbing all of the marvels and new places of interest on that side of the street. She did catch sight of the elderly woman but she didn't pay attention until she heard, "Well hello there young lady."

That voice was unforgettable, while it had many years mastered into it, without needing to wonder, Delores knew immediately who was calling out to her.

In a quarter half turn, Delores turned and said, "Are you talking to me?"

In a soft voice, Mother Montgomery said, "You and I are the only two on this street sweetheart."

Delores' posture slumped slightly while she rubbed the corner of her eyelid, she stood thinking, "*Is this really happening to me right now? I'm not in town a good hour and the first person I run into is this old bitty? Will someone please give me a freaking break; I need several.*"

In an attempt to engage in small talk, Mother Montgomery offered Delores a compliment, "You look well dear, how have you been?"

Delores shot back saying, "Oh you want to know how I've been since you ran me out of town? Is that what you want to know?"

Mother Montgomery raised her hands up in her defense and said, "I can see you are still carrying this and I didn't mean to upset you. I saw you walking down the street and I wanted to come and greet you." Speaking under her breath, Mother Montgomery looked up at Delores and said, "Did you come here for him?"

Delores' veins pulsed to the near point of engorgement, with sweeping arm gestures, she said, "You have got to be kidding me? I know you didn't just ask me that." Deliberately making inflammatory statements said, "You wicked and evil woman, how dare you ask me such a thing after you killed my relationship with your son. You knew nothing about me, didn't even try and without thinking you crushed him without giving any consideration as to his feelings."

Defending her position, trying to appeal to Delores' sensibilities, Mother Montgomery said, "Listen, listen I did what I saw my husband's mother do, I was chosen, my husband didn't pick me and yet we had a loving marriage."

In an aggressive tone, Delores sunk to deep levels of pettiness and insults, she said, "Do you think I care about what you saw someone else do. You were in complete control of that situation and you chose to handle that the way you wanted. You should just admit you didn't think I was good enough for your family. The thing is, at the time, the little my parents had was more than you could have ever possessed. You took advantage of my mother's illness and used it as leverage to destroy my relationship with your son. But you know what, God keeps track of the decent folks." Delores unloaded all of the bottled up emotion she'd carried over the years onto Mother Montgomery. Without backing down, she said, "And now you want to know if I'm here for him? Oh how the tables have turned. Back then in your offices, I looked at you and your husband through lens filled with fear and intimidation. Now I look at you and I see nothing. Lady, you are like a joke with no punchline, a slapstick figure in a moral circus. You need to go and have several seats."

As an intended consequence, Delores was causing a scene outside of the restaurant, Lillian walked out to see about Mother Montgomery, she said, "Is everything alright out here?"

Mother Montgomery responded, "Yes, Lillian, all is well. I'll be back inside shortly."

Hoping to make amends, Mother Montgomery said, "Just like you've been carrying this all of these years, so have I. I'm up in age and wherever I can make apologies and ask for forgiveness, I want to be able to do that. I'm sorry for what I did and I hope you can get to a place where you can let this go because listen…he needs you. Yes, Regina was my girl, my choice but he picked you. Now that she's gone, all kind of women are trying to get at him and I don't like that. I know you lost your husband not too long ago and so you two can be a source of support for one another. You two now suddenly have a chance to have a real relationship, it's like the two of you have struck a windfall or hit a real life bonanza. Listen to me, I don't know why you're here or how long you plan to stay and I know I'm in no position to ask anything of you but while you are here, will you reach out to him. I know he'd be happy to see you and I hope in some small way, you can get some peace from what happened."

Listening to Mother Montgomery, Delores felt a sudden stroke of divine justice, the apology raised years of resentment from her life. She looked at Mother Montgomery and said, "I already have an abundance of peace that you could never give to me. Without committing to anything, Delores said without walking away, "But I do thank you for the apology."

CHAPTER 39

The bright rays of sunlight cascaded through the blinds of Bishop's room. With a second heartbeat hammering away in his head, Bishop rolled over and held onto the sides of his head in an effort to quiet the noise. He woke up trying to figure out how he'd ended up in the bed with no clothes on. The vapors from his late night liquid sins seeped out of every pore of his body granting him secondary inebriation.

The itinerary he'd been given the night before indicated breakfast was being served but because his body had lost the ability to create saliva, he felt like his tongue could quite possibly suffocate him so eating breakfast wasn't going to be an option. Pajamas and slippers seemed to be what the daily special had to offer.

Despite the harrowing pangs of his inaugural hangover, Bishop still felt like it felt better than the sorrow he felt.

He wanted to enjoy the communal energy of the roundtable breakfasts but his pure system didn't take kindly to being defiled by the devil's firewater.

Barely able to lift his head, he turned on his back to look up as if to search for the Lord. He gazed at the ceiling and said, "Father, forgive me for right now, I know not what I'm doing. In a moment of weakness, I spiraled down a rabbit hole of despair but I know I can't live like this. As your servant, I want to have clean hands when I stand before your people so help me Lord to make it through this season in my life. As hard as it seems, I'm going to trust You."

While he laid in bed weeping, a free flow of gourmet and bounteous delights were being served. At The Bolts, breakfast, the first meal of the day was considered a celebration and the food selections matched the occasion.

Dottie was moving about, acting hyper and unable to keep still, she was on level ten, ready and waiting to finally see her sister, Delores.

Walking into the dining area, Dottie caught a glimpse of Delores as she was darting in and out of the kitchen.

Placing a fresh batch of homemade, buttery golden brown croissants down on the table, Dottie ran over to Delores jumping up and down smiling saying, "You're here, you're here...I can't believe you're finally here."

Delores smirked and said, "I'm not so sure why it's so hard for you to believe, you and everyone else practically harassed the dickens out of me until I felt like I had no other choice but to come. So yes, now I'm here."

The two sisters laughed and hugged one another.

Dottie usually worked at the inn during the daytime hours and other family members worked in the evening and at night so she was already gone when Delores arrived the night before.

Dottie had never been able to keep anything so grabbing onto Delores' arm, she held onto it and without wasting much time she whispered, "He's here Dee."

Trying to fix a plate of breakfast, Delores shot a quick glance at her sister and asked, "Who's here?"

Dottie's eyes glowed with inner light, she perked up and said, "Eugene Montgomery is here...he's staying here at the inn. He's on the registry under an alias but I got a call from a friend who wanted him to come here and get away for a while."

Losing her appetite, Delores placed her untouched food down on the table, her face went slack and she closed her eyes saying, "I knew this was a bad idea. This is too much, I'm not real sure what's going on here but I'm not getting ready to be a part of it. I've come too far to turn around now."

Dottie pursed her lips together and titled her head in her sister's direction saying, "I'm confused. What are you talking about?"

Delores filled in Dottie on the details regarding her meeting with Mother Montgomery.

Dottie shuffled back and step and gasped.

"Oh my goodness, you said all of that her to Delores?" Dottie asked.

Nodding her head, Delores said, "I sure did and it felt good. I think I must've had an adrenaline rush after each low blow I said but now I feel horrible about it. I should've never talked to that woman that way. Its old stuff and she's old and I guess I just let the situation get the best of me."

Dottie picked up Delores' plate and said, "You need to eat." Turning serious for a moment, Dottie said, "By you responding to her the way you did, that says to me, there's a wound there or something…maybe there's something still there between you two. I mean, would you have reacted to his mother that way if there wasn't."

Any appetite she'd gained, she lost it again at Dottie's questions. Delores put the plate back down and said, "Too much time has passed. Like I said, too much old stuff, I'm not interested in getting tangled up with that family anymore. I learned a long time ago, if you don't fit into their nice and neat little box and serve their purposes, you're no good to them and I'm not interested in living my life like that. As we all know, life is too short."

Dottie probed a bit further, "I agree, life is too short but what if life has brought you two back to the place where you can put the past behind you and start over again?"

Delores grabbed onto her sister's arm and said, "I know you mean well but please let's not push the issue. You wanted me here so we can take care of the business of the inn and you said you wanted to spend some time together so let's do that and not talk about this. If I'm going to be here doing those things, I'm not going to stay here as long as he is; I'll be checking out today and staying somewhere else until he leaves."

"I don't know why you aren't staying with me anyway." Dottie said.

"I've never stayed here so I thought if I was going to come here and see about it I might as well experience it for myself right?" Delores replied.

Backing off and honoring her sister's wishes, Dottie, said, "Alright Delores, I hear you…welcome home sis."

CHAPTER 40

Karen walked up to Carson's bedroom to check his vitals, it was like a miracle, with each day, his condition was slightly improving. Rebekkah had awaken earlier that morning and was downstairs watching television.

Logging his blood pressure reading into the system, Karen reached over and tossed Carson an envelope saying, "Here are those test results you wanted, they were able to do it within like twenty-four hours."

Staring at the envelope, Carson contemplated whether he wanted to open it and find out its contents.

With Karen being there daily, she agreed to also care for Rebekkah while she recovered from the gunshot wound. Under the guise of doctor's orders, she was able to obtain a blood sample from her and she collected a swap from Carson and sent it off to the lab for an in-utero, prenatal paternity test.

From the moment Rebekkah returned, he'd had his doubts but he couldn't prove anything so he went along and bought what Rebekkah was selling him.

Karen left him alone and announced she'd be back to check on him later.

Tracing over the logo on the envelope Carson made himself believe there was no way anyone else could be the father of Rebekkah's baby.

The only way he could be one hundred percent certain was to open the test and check the results.

Sitting on the edge of the bed, beads of sweat started to form around his forehead, he used the envelope to fan himself.

The fear of the unknown overwhelmed him, this baby was his chance to start over and be better and to have that ideal and opportunity threatened was more than he could handle. He ripped up the test and tossed it in the trash. He quickly walked out of his room.

Halfway down the hall, he turned around and ran back into the room and knelt down by the wastebasket. Piecing the papers back together, trembled at what his eyes saw. He felt like he was on an episode of *Maury Povich,* where the pronouncement was made, "Carson Eugene Montgomery IV, YOU ARE NOT THE FATHER."

Carson crumbled under the burden of proof that with ninety-nine percent accuracy he wasn't the father of Rebekkah's baby.

He sat unnaturally still on the floor as he tried to figure out his next move. Rebekkah walked in before his brain could finish its processing and as a result he wasn't in his right frame of mind and that was apparent.

Rebekkah knelt down beside him and said, "Carson, are you alright, did you fall or something?"

"I had a downfall." He said.

"Huh? Let me help you up." She offered.

Snatching his hand away from her, he said, "Get your nasty behind hands off of me you stanking, low-class, no-class whore."

Carson had rendered Rebekkah speechless, bowled over and knocked for six, she stood trying to understand what was going on.

"Oh, don't stand there like you don't know what I'm talking about." He shouted.

"Carson, I have no idea what's going on with you right now." She declared.

With both barrels blazing he came straight out and asked, "Is that my baby you're carrying?"

Jerking her head back, she said, "But of course it is silly, who else would it be?"

Flicking the papers in her face, he said, "Well this test says otherwise and I'd venture to say Godfrey is the lucky man."

Rebekkah held the torn pieces of paper in her hands and let them drop to the floor saying, "Well, this test is wrong, this test isn't right Carson…this is your baby. You and I created this baby together, in love."

Standing up and getting his bearing, Carson turned and punched a hole in the wall, he screamed, "My mother knew you were bad news and she tried over and over to warn me to open my eyes to you but I was dazzled and blinded by what you did for me and how you made me feel. Now, I'm standing here knowing you apparently made Godfrey feel the same way."

Maintaining her story, Rebekkah said, "Now Carson, I've made a lot of mistakes in my life but I assure you this isn't one of them. You showed me that men sometimes do leave their wives and now you and I are trying to reconcile and we're going to have a baby." Placing his hand on her stomach, she said, "This is your baby Carson."

Downstairs, Karen heard the cussing and the fussing and determined the nature of the argument. She waited for a few minutes but the arguing grew louder and more intense with each passing minute. She placed a call to Bishop Montgomery, he didn't answer. She tried calling Christian, he didn't answer either. She figured the next call would be a long shot but she tried it anyway. She dialed Regina's number, she thought maybe someone might have her phone and whoever had it could get over there right away. In an effort to protect the family, she didn't want to have to call the police.

On the other end of Regina's phone, Bishop Montgomery answered.

He'd turned his phone off but he kept Regina's phone to play back her voice recordings so he could hear her voice again.

In hurried speech, Karen whizzed by and related to Bishop what was going on and encouraged him to hurry and get over to the house.

Rushing to get himself together, Bishop grabbed a shirt and pants and did a quick swish in his mouth with toothpaste and water. He picked up his keys and dashed out of the door. Focused on getting to Carson's, he wasn't paying attention when he tripped over a foot at the valet stand. A disheveled Bishop Montgomery toppled down to the ground.

The foot belonged to none other than Delores Bolton Cartwright. She was seated on the bench outside waiting for her car so she could go over to her sister's house. She was reading a book, _The Love Bug_ by an author she'd heard about, Shakira R. Thompson so she didn't see Bishop barreling down the sidewalk so she could move her feet in time.

The book fell on his head and she along with the other valet drivers tried to help him up off the ground.

He looked up and said, "Delores?" Thinking he still might have been drunk he felt like he must have been hallucinating.

With a darting glance, she said, "Yes, it's me."

Bishop's ears turned red, his heart skipped a beat, and he felt flutters in his stomach, he sat down on the ground and shook his head saying, "This is too much; I don't know how much more of this I can take."

Delores could barely look at him, in spite of apparent aging and recovering from being three sheets to the wind, Bishop Montgomery was just as handsome as he was the day she met him.

He jumped up and said, "This is going to sound real crazy but I have an emergency situation going on with my son but I can't believe I just tripped over your feet. If there is such a thing, I'm literally tripping over you. Will you please come go with me, I haven't seen you in so long and I'd like to talk to you and catch up. Plus, I could use some reinforcement considering what's going on over at my son's house."

Delores could feel his strain and the pull was too great for her to turn him down, she agreed to ride and the valet pulled up, they got in his car.

Bishop Montgomery placed a call to Karen to let her know he was on the way. She pleaded with him to get there as fast as he could.

Upstairs, Carson was still carrying on and Karen heard him say, "Yeah, how about that, I left my wife for you. I kicked her out, I didn't even know she was pregnant. Here I was thinking it was you but she was indeed the chosen one, she's the one who has given me a son and because of you, now another man is raising my child in some Podunk town in Mississippi."

Reaching into the night stand, Carson pulled out the gun he'd accidentally shot Rebekkah with. He waved it in the air and pointed it at her, he looked at her and said, "I didn't mean to shoot you the first time but this time you're going to die tonight."

Backing away with her hand in front of her acting as a shield, through tears, Rebekkah pleaded, "Carson, you don't mean that. Put the gun away. You don't want to do something you're going to regret later."

Aiming the gun in Rebekkah's direction he said, "I've already done something I regret…hooking up with you. My mother didn't get a chance to see my baby and now she's dead." He screamed even louder, "Do you hear me, she's dead." Turning the gun towards himself, he said, "Instead of killing you, maybe I should join her. Maybe, I should just rid myself of myself and make life easier for everyone."

Crying her eyes out, Rebekkah begged him, "Carson please don't do this."

Standing by the door, Karen tapped her feet anxiously waiting for Bishop Montgomery to show up. As she opened the door for him and Delores to come in they heard a gunshot followed by screams.

Delores, Karen, and Bishop all ran upstairs to the bedroom. They rushed in and saw Rebekkah on the floor with her hand covering her head bawling and squalling while Carson had the gun down by his side.

He'd fired off a shot for dramatic effect.

CHAPTER 41

"I'm sorry you had to witness all of that but thank you for coming with me today."

Delores sipped a drink of water and said, "You don't have to apologize, your family is going through a tough time, I know all too well about that. I'm glad I could be here for you."

Bishop Montgomery looked at Delores and said, "I feel like I'm losing it. I've been trying to keep it together but so much is happening I think I'm fighting a losing battle. My kids are angry, my church is wounded, and I don't know if I'm coming or going."

Noticing Delores had been guarded around him he felt like he'd keep the conversation on him and try not to pry too much into her life until she was ready. He was appreciative of her time and conversation, he was happy to be talking to anyone and he was especially pleased it was her.

The server placed their food on the table and Bishop said a blessing over their meal and their fellowship.

Delores took a bite and then said, "Do you think Carson and Rebekkah are going to be okay?"

Bishop took a forkful of his food and then said, "Carson has always been a bit of a hot head, once he cools down, he'll be able to think straight. I couldn't believe he fired that gun, even if it was to scare her, we could have been having a different kind of conversation right now had someone gotten hurt. However, I think having him come out there with me at your family's inn will do him some good. Which I have to say, by the way, I did not make the connection that the Bolton's owned The Bolt." Bishop chuckled. "Thank you for setting that up for him Delores, I really appreciate that. I'm not sure where Rebekkah is going to end up. Before we left, I heard Carson say he was about to call his attorney to get the divorce proceedings started and he also mentioned he needed to know about adoptions or something like that he said. I'm not sure what he meant by that but prayerfully everything will work itself out."

Delores decided to keep her vulnerabilities hiding from her first love, she tried hard to fight against the quiver in her heart. Whether she was willing to admit it or not, the feelings she once had for Bishop Montgomery were still there, they hadn't gone anywhere, she'd only repressed them.

He watched her as her eyes glowed against the candlelight. The sun was setting and the restaurant was adjusting the lighting for their dinner service by turning down the lights and lighting the candles.

Bishop Montgomery thought back on the days prior to Regina when his heart burned for Delores like the fire in the votive on their table.

He accidently brushed up against her hand and they both felt the sparks of electricity, he smiled, she frowned.

When their server came to introduce dessert, Delores declined and said, "This has been nice but I think we should make it back to the inn."

Not wanting to get on her bad side, Bishop took care of the check after she insisted on paying for her portion, he said, "Accept this as my thank you for helping me out today."

On the way back to the inn, he asked, "So how long are you planning to be here."

In a closed off posture, she said, "I'm not sure."

In a softened voice, he said, "Well, if it's alright, I'd like to see you again, just to talk of course, before you leave."

Pulling up to the inn she hopped out of the car and said, "We'll see. Thanks for the early dinner and I hope everything works out okay with your family."

Walking away from the car, Delores struggled against turning around to see him one more time, she walked inside the inn thinking to herself, *"Oh my God, I'm still in love with Eugene Montgomery and I'm not so sure how I feel about that."*

Bishop Montgomery checked on Carson before retiring to his room for the evening he thought back on his time with Delores and thought, *"Is it wrong for me to admit that she still has my heart so soon after my Regina has passed?"*

EPILOGUE

"Regina has gone on to be with the Lord and Delores has returned. Can you all believe what has happened to me and my family within this last month? Have to wonder are you all praying for your Bishop, do you really pray for me?"

"Throughout my life, I've gone through many ups and downs, several trials and tribulations but I need to let you know that Regina dying has probably been the toughest thing in my life to deal with. I feel a tremendous amount of guilt and honestly that is what hurts. Regina was fulfilling the call of God on her life, she tapped in her purpose and the plan God had for her and I was too insecure to see that. I felt neglected and I had a hard time sharing her with the world."

"My dear brothers and sisters if you have loved ones and you have the chance, hug them more, kiss them longer, tell them you love them frequently, all while giving them the opportunity to spread their wings and do what God sent them here to do. I know Regina is in heaven rejoicing and I couldn't be happier for her, this is what we live our lives for. I'm just going to miss her and I already miss her dearly."

"Now that Delores is back, I'm struggling with what I should do if I should do anything. Do you all think I should at least try to see if we can reconnect or rekindle the love we once shared? The problem is, I have been out of the dating game for a long time so I need some advice. I believe having a second chance with her would feel like what winning the lottery must be like. Having her back in my life feels like I've already hit the jackpot, especially after I feel like mourning the loss of my wife has taken me to rock bottom."

"If you have any ideas, recommendations, or advice on how I should handle things going forward with Delores, email me at shakirabelieves@gmail.com with the subject, Advice for Bishop and help me out, I'd greatly appreciate any and all input and feedback. Be blessed my brothers and sisters, I look forward to hearing from you all soon."

The Big Bonanza
Psalms 37:11

"Before you know it, the wicked will have had it; you'll stare at his once famous place and – nothing. Down-to-earth people will move in and take over, relishing a huge bonanza." (MSG)

About the Author

Shakira R. Thompson, a natural born storyteller who submitted to her God-given talents and in doing so, God showed up and made her a BELIEVER. He's transformed her into an author, publisher, and entrepreneur.

She is the founder of Believer's Choice Media, an inspirational content company dedicated to encouraging believers to live the life they were created to live on earth and beyond. She's penned five, well-received inspirational fiction novels with a sixth on the way.

With a renewed sense of purpose, Shakira is not only writing and speaking, she's living...living her life according to Ephesians 2:10:

"For we are his workmanship, created in Christ Jesus unto good works, which God hath before ordained that we should walk in them." (KJV)

Shakira is a proud Alumni of Florida A&M University in Tallahassee, Florida where she holds a B.S in Business Administration as well as an M.B.A. with a concentration in Supply Chain Management.

Shakira has always delved in the world of real estate, but most recently made it official. She is a Realtor®, licensed in the State of Florida, where she's the listing agent for EquityPro. Naturally, she' s expanding the Believer's Choice brand and is in the process of developing Believer's Choice Realty, LLC.

Living her life with purpose has pushed her into her latest venture, co-hosting *The Dee Lee Show,* where she has the opportunity to encourage **BELIEVERS** over the airwaves.

Although Shakira may wear many hats these days, the most important role to her, is that of wife and mother.

Born and raised in Fernandina Beach, Florida, she now resides in Orlando, Florida with her family.

A Sneak Peek
The Empowerment Circle

Malynda Monroe took a deep breath as she walked onto the platform. As she stepped onto the platform, the light blinded her. Her heart pounded and her breathing was course. She was certain that everybody in the church could see the beads of sweat dripping off of her.

"I have pull myself together," Malynda thought to herself.

Malynda stood with the microphone in her hand, awaiting the coming wave of sorrow that was flooding her. It washed over her as a rushing waterfall. How had her life gotten to this point?

Up until two months before, Malynda had everything going for her – she had an international ministry, she was the author of over seventy inspirational books, her voice was heard all over the world – even the secular media had her on for interviews. She had handled the ministry perfectly, kept meticulous books upon each dollar that was spent in the ministry; she never wanted to be one of those ministers that had a dramatic fall due to the lack of financial accountability.

However, all that changed when an agent from the IRS, agent Harrison Sinclair came to her house one day and told her that her financial records had been wrong. He told her that there was evidence of concealed bank accounts, excessive personal expenditures, payments to fictitious people, among a laundry list of other things and that the case was being referred to the Criminal Investigation Division.

Agent Sinclair informed Malynda that her ministry, *Mercy Light,* was involved in illegal financial activities and when fraud is detected, the IRS can go back six years rather than the intended three to uncover illegal activity and assess additional taxes and penalties. Given the size and magnitude of the ministry, they were given the latitude needed to investigate the ministry only to uncover that for the last eleven years, *Mercy Light Ministries* was suspected of the mismanagement of funds.

Malynda immediately placed a call to her attorneys and her husband's financial firm to find out what was going on and how she was to respond. Shocked and confused, Malynda knew that she was innocent, that she had never stolen anyone's money. What she didn't understand was how this was even possible considering that her husband, co-founder of *Mercy Light Ministries*, had taken care of the finances of the ministry until his untimely death in a tragic car accident six months prior. Before going into ministry, Randall Monroe was a Certified Public Accountant and his firm performed financial management and oversight to nonprofit organizations, churches, and ministries. It was through his associations and relationships that starting a ministry would be perfect for them. When they founded the ministry, it was no question that Monroe and Associates would handle the finances of the ministry.

Agent Sinclair had a personal interest in this case because he had grown up watching his grandmother give the little bit of money she had to preachers on the television and not getting anything in return.

Malynda had never seen any of the finances that were placed into the ministry because she had full faith and trust in her husband and his company. When her husband passed away, it was written in his will that his firm would continue to manage the funds of the ministry. She was completely innocent. Malynda was still reeling from the news and in a state of confusion when her attorneys, the

Johnson brothers showed up at her door along with a representative from Randall and Associates.

Malynda greeted everyone and asked them to come into the living room where Agent Sinclair was seated. He stood and shook hands with everyone. Malynda asked Agent Sinclair to inform the gentlemen of the charges and what she was facing.

Agent Sinclair, repeated the same things to the men that he had said to Malynda earlier but ended by saying, "In some cases that are being referred to the Criminal Investigation Division, the referral can be made null and void if the suspect comes clean."

It was clear to everyone in the room that the only available options were, either go to jail because of the overwhelming evidence or come clean and pay the fines.

Malynda thought to herself, *"This is the deal I'm being offered, confess to the crimes I didn't commit or go to jail for crimes I didn't commit."*

She was to be the fall guy for somebody in her ministry that was not whom they said they were.

Looking to Dante and Darrell, her attorneys for answers with tears in her eyes, "What should I do?" Malynda said, "I didn't do this; you both know that I didn't do this."

She looked at the representative, Kevin Greggory from her deceased husband's firm, "How do you explain this, tell me how this could have happened!"

They all stood there with no words as Malynda tried to find the words to describe what she was thinking and what she was going to do.

The three men, the two brothers, Dante and Darrell, and Kevin looked at each other and then grabbed Malynda by the hand and in unison said, "Take the deal."

"What." Malynda shouted at them, "You want me to do what? As God is my witness, I never stole any money from anyone and you have no proof that I did any of this." Malynda said as she paced the floor.

With her hands covering her chest as if to protect her heart from shattering into little pieces on the floor where she stood, she said, "My ministry has always been about giving to people, not taking from them."

Agent Sinclair spoke up and said, "Mrs. Monroe, unfortunately, whether you did the stealing or your ministry, it's all one in the same to us. You do have a choice here, just come clean that your ministry stole money from hard-working people and we can make this all disappear.

"What about me not stealing money don't you seem to get, Agent Sinclair?" Malynda shouted.

Trying to calm her down, Dante and Darrel sat her down on the sofa and Dante said, "Malynda, take his deal. It's for the best… think about the kids and the ministry."

Dante knelt down by her and said, "The kids have already lost their father, you don't want them to lose their mother either, do you?"

Darrell leaned into her and said, "Everyone has been through so much since Randall Sr. passed away, let's not add any unnecessary stress on everyone, take the deal."

Thinking over how things had been since her husband passed away and the thought of leaving her children if she went to jail caused Malynda to say with reluctance, "Okay, I'll take the deal but I did not do this."

Smiling at her agreeing to confess, Agent Sinclair said, "I know that you are scheduled for a large conference in two months and I believe that the best way for you to make your confession will be there in front of all of your adoring fans." He continued on to say, "My agency will work with your administration and your attorneys to work out the details for the announcement that will take place in two months." As he gathered his things to leave, he said to Malynda, "You've made the right decision and I will be watching when you make your announcement."

The Empowerment Circle

Note from the Author
Final Thoughts

I consider myself to be a Christian Fiction Romance writer or even an Inspirational novelist, which means that strong Christian themes and scriptures are strewn throughout each of my stories. However, I've been told that while each story has strong faithful ties because they hold universal truths anyone can relate to them.

It is my prayer that as you read these stories that you find these sentiments to be true, that you are able to relate to them and you find them to be a blessing.

My dear brothers and sisters, life can bring forth many surprises, some welcomed and some not so much, however, whatever season you may find yourself in, never forget to put your total and complete trust in Him.

One Last Thing....

If you've enjoyed this book and any of the others and believe your family and friends would enjoy it as well, I'd be honored if you decided to spread the word and tell them about it.

I'd also be forever grateful if you took a minute to post a review where ever you hang out online, whether by social media, Amazon, Goodreads, or Smashwords, you get the idea.

For more information about what's going on with me, for latest news and announcements, book updates, simply ready to believe and so much more, please head over to www.shakirabelieves.com and sign up.

Shakira R. Thompson

All the best,

~ *Shakira*

www.ingramcontent.com/pod-product-compliance
Lightning Source LLC
Chambersburg PA
CBHW051251250626
47155CB00009B/3261